"Sometimes, I just talk and stupid things happen. Like yesterday, I was telling Dalia about the library—"

"You told your sister about yesterday?" My heart pops like a firecracker.

"Well"—he takes off his baseball cap—"it was kind of hard to hide this at the dinner table." He leans forward to show me the knot on his head.

"Wow. I did that." Without thinking, I touch the knot and feel terribly guilty (and slightly satisfied) when Danny flinches.

"Yeah, did you have to choose the unabridged dictionary? Couldn't you have just used your pocket Webster?" His dimples appear. I want to rub my finger in the indent.

"What did you tell your sister?" I am curious. I've never had my name pass between the lips of the socially elite.

"I don't know. I just told her some stuff. So why did you throw the book at me?"

Good question. Too bad I didn't have one good, rational answer. "I don't know. You were there with this 'I don't care that I'm late' attitude."

"Sometimes the coach keeps us late."

At this point, he could tell me that he likes green eggs and ham. I don't care. I'm stuck somewhere between understanding that our knees are touching and that he, too, washes his face with Neutrogena. I can smell it on him. . . .

# NOT anything

### CARMEN
### rodrigues

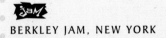

BERKLEY JAM, NEW YORK

**THE BERKLEY PUBLISHING GROUP**
**Published by the Penguin Group**
**Penguin Group (USA) Inc.**
**375 Hudson Street, New York, New York 10014, USA**
Penguin Group (Canada), 90 Eglinton Avenue East, Suite 700, Toronto, Ontario M4P 2Y3, Canada
(a division of Pearson Penguin Canada Inc.)
Penguin Books Ltd., 80 Strand, London WC2R 0RL, England
Penguin Group Ireland, 25 St. Stephen's Green, Dublin 2, Ireland (a division of Penguin Books Ltd.)
Penguin Group (Australia), 250 Camberwell Road, Camberwell, Victoria 3124, Australia
(a division of Pearson Australia Group Pty. Ltd.)
Penguin Books India Pvt. Ltd., 11 Community Centre, Panchsheel Park, New Delhi—110 017, India
Penguin Group (NZ), 67 Apollo Drive, Rosedale, North Shore 0632, New Zealand
(a division of Pearson New Zealand Ltd.)
Penguin Books (South Africa) (Pty.) Ltd., 24 Sturdee Avenue, Rosebank, Johannesburg 2196,
South Africa

Penguin Books Ltd., Registered Offices: 80 Strand, London WC2R 0RL, England

NOT ANYTHING

This book is an original publication of The Berkley Publishing Group.

PRINTING HISTORY
Berkley JAM trade paperback edition / February 2008

Berkley JAM trade paperback ISBN: 978-0-425-21928-7

An application to register this book for cataloging has been submitted to the Library of Congress.

PRINTED IN THE UNITED STATES OF AMERICA

10  9  8  7  6  5  4  3  2

For David

# ACKNOWLEDGMENTS

• • •

I lost a close family friend in the months before I began writing *Not Anything*. What surprised me the most about my grief was that it was so vast. It didn't hit all at once, instead it appeared at the most inopportune times—the red light two blocks from home, the bathroom at work. I found from talking to more-experienced mourners that my grief would last for years. And eventually—if I made the effort—I could learn to adjust to its quake.

It was then that I began to write *Not Anything*, a novel in which a teenage girl struggles to deal with the loss of her mother five years before, emotional isolation from her father, high school, and the intimidating task of falling in love at the tender age of fifteen.

This was an ambitious project for me, and from the novel's conception to the point of publication, I received tremendous support. So without further ado, I'd like to thank:

Caren Lissner, for giving me my first writing gig, encouraging the writing of this novel, and offering me sound advice.

My teachers—specifically Mrs. Johnson and Mr. Strickland (Sunset Senior High), and Dr. Berry and Mary Jane Ryals (FSU)—for helping me to become a better writer and human being.

All the kids I went to high school with for giving me stories to tell and romances to re-create.

YA authors Stephanie Hale and Bethany Griffin, for navigating this unpredictable journey with me. Your feedback and encouragement mean the world to me.

All the YA authors at teenlitauthors@yahoogroups.com, particularly Alesia Holliday (a.k.a. Jax Abbott), for starting this group.

Agent Rachel Vater, for being kind enough to pass along my manuscript.

My own determined (and insanely gorgeous) agent Zoe Fishman, for reading said manuscript, declaring it loveable, and taking on the tremendous task of finding it a good home! Infinite thanks!

The rest of my Lowenstein-Yost Associates family, particularly Barbara Lowenstein and Nancy Yost, for embracing my work and launching my career.

Kate Seaver, my editor at Berkley Books, for believing in this story, giving me my first big break, and not suggesting that I change the title or the ending. I applaud you!

Allison Brandau, Kate's solid right hand, for answering all my "newbie" questions with a cheerful attitude.

Prescott Tolk, comedian extraordinaire, for pushing me "to reach for the moon."

Michelle Civile and Brian McCann, for being the two best "civilian" friends a girl could ever have. I love you both so much.

And, most important, to my family: Mom, for taking me to the library and telling me that you loved me; Natalie, for the unique bedtime stories that fed my imagination; my real-life Suzi, for always pushing me forward. You are my "best-est" friend and my reader of choice; and Walter, for surviving a family of bossy girls and loving us, despite our shortcomings.

## acknowledgments

   I'd also like to thank my extended family: John, Trevor, Isiah, Savannah, Jenna, Nathanial, Grandma Monse, and Grandpa Ramón. Your personal stories are mine to tell.

   And to David Jason Ashworth, whose tragic death led me to write this story: you are missed. Always.

# ONE

# the yearbook picture line

* * *

holding up a school line is dangerous business.

The worst part is that I've done all that I can to make this experience end. I've given Fred, the photographer, the slight curve-of-the-lip-closed-mouth sneer, the half-open/half-closed-mouth grimace, the mysterious-faced Mona Lisa, and anything else that might possibly pass as a smile, and . . . nothing. We're on our fourth shot, and he keeps saying that he'll take my yearbook picture over and over again until I smile—get this—happily.

The problem is that I haven't smiled for a yearbook picture since the fourth grade, and I'm pretty sure that it's not going to happen now. But that's not going to stop me from having a panic attack. That's my specialty. I've been having those since the sixth grade. And here it is—

- ☑ Shortness of breath

- ☑ Pain across my chest

- ☑ Uncontrollable body movements

"Just breathe, Susie," Marisol whispers from the opposite side of the room.

"Yeah, dipshit, breathe," Billy Wilson adds from behind her. "And stop looking so stupid!"

"God." Marisol gives Billy a dirty look "What is your problem?" She turns back to me and says, "Just think of . . ." before she takes this God-awful long pause that hangs there for all eternity. This gives Billy several more opportunities to make funny faces at me, so I tell myself to tune him out and think. Think. What can I think of?

I can think of . . . stupid songs. Like? *Just what makes that little ole ant think he'll move that rubber tree plant?*

No. No. No. I haven't sunk so low that I need to pep myself up with silly, encouraging songs.

*What else?*

I guess I can think of . . . Marisol? Like what's up with the long pause? Okay, unsafe territory.

*What else? What else?*

I can think of . . . my father? But what do I know about my father? Of course *I know* him, but what do I know *about* him except for the fact that he'll spend less than ten minutes a day talking to me because that's enough time to catch up on my very unimportant life. Again, unsafe territory.

*What else is there? Who else is there?*

My grandma? I love her, but she keeps forgetting my name.

*What else?*

What's the point of my high IQ if I can't think under pressure?

*Wait. Wait. Something's coming.*

*Something is . . .* Yes! I can think about my next class. Mr. Murphy's class, a.k.a. English class, a.k.a. my favorite class at Orange Grove Senior High. And right now we're reading *Pride and Prejudice*. Ah, Jane Austen.

Yes! This is a safe one! I love Jane Austen. And I like Mr. Murphy. He's always nice. Like last week when Jason Solocone made fun of the way I pronounced, or should I say mispronounced—

*Ca-raaap!*

Mr. Murphy was so nice to me last week that I agreed to begin tutoring for him. *Today?* TODAY!

And here comes the twitch—right back where I left it. And here come their voices—right back where I left them, only now they're like wind-tunnel voices. I feel like I'm going to keel over from the weight of everything. Everything is slo-mo and excruciating.

Marisol says, *"Gaaaaawd, I duuuuunno. Just smiiiiile allllre-addddy."*

Billy says, *"Seeeeeee, Daaaaannyyyy, sheeeee's tootaallyyy twiiiitchiiiing—"*

And it's after that exchange that I try to find something to hold on to so I don't go and blow away with the wind. I think, *Danny? Isn't that the name of the guy that I'm tutoring?* And it is, so I start to list facts about him in my head because sometimes listing things that are concrete makes me feel calm. And right now, I need to feel calm.

So here are the facts about Danny Diaz. He's:

1. A junior

2. A varsity soccer player

3. Extremely popular

4. A twin—His twin sister is Dalia Diaz, the only junior to ever be named head of the school's dance team, the Sun-Kissed Girls.

The list is super-short. I have to go over the facts several times before the wind tunnel disappears, and I can look past Billy Wilson—and his manic need to destroy any shred of self-confidence that I have—toward the guy standing directly behind him. The one watching me. And I wonder if it can be? (Because that would be too much of a ridiculous coincidence.) But can it be?

And that's when our eyes lock and the guy-who-might-be-Danny says gently, "Just smile, Susie." And then he does the strangest thing, the least expected thing. He smiles at me.

I mean, I think he smiles at me. I can't be sure because everyone's speaking all at once.

Billy says, "That's what I'm talking about. Feisty dykes. That's hot." Then, he blows me a kiss.

Marisol says, "Just smile," for, like, the twentieth time.

The photographer says, "Hold on, just got to change the battery."

By the time I let my eyes drift back to the guy-who-might-be-Danny, his face is such a complete void that I'm not even sure he smiled at me at all.

"Okay." The photographer pops the new battery into his fancy digital camera. "Let's try that again."

And so that's what we do. We try it over and over and over again. And I never get it right, because I can't smile.

# TWO

# danny diaz

* * *

when i'm nervous, i laugh. that's a fact. the first time it happened was when I was nine. I was peering into my mother's coffin when, just like that, I laughed.

Not that my mother's death has anything to do with this.

Yeah, I feel nervous. Yeah, I want to laugh. But that's where the similarities end. Like I said, my mother's death is in no way equal to this stupid meeting. It just reminds me of her funeral, that's all. That happens sometimes. My brain makes weird connections like that.

See, it's like even though it hasn't happened yet, I know how bad this meeting—this tutoring situation—with Danny Diaz is going to turn out. I know because I know. That's all. I know because I know how boys are with me. I know how boys are with me because . . . well, where do I start?

Marc Sanchez.

Marc Sanchez is my neighbor, and I hate everything about him. I hate when his stupid friends pick him up in the morning. I hate when he hangs out under the palm trees in front of his house with his stupid girlfriend. I hate when I see him sneaking out to the side of his house to smoke pot.

But you want to know what I really hate about Marc Sanchez? I hate that I know everything about him. I know that he's got a birthmark shaped like the state of Texas on the back of his thigh. I know that the scar underneath his eyebrow is from when we were seven and he fell off his dad's truck. (Okay, I pushed him, but we were playing.) I know that the freckles on his face—yes, those twenty thousand freckles—don't just stop there. They go everywhere.

But you want to know what I really, really hate about Marc Sanchez? That one day Marc woke up and had a thought that went something like this: "Today I'm going to ignore Susie and act like she doesn't exist." And that's pretty much what he did. It was the end of our fourth-grade year and, like that, I disappeared.

"Well . . ." Mr. Murphy clears his throat. "Danny, may I present to you Miss Susie Shannon. Susie," Mr. Murphy turns to me, "may I present to you Mr. Danny Diaz."

Before we get started, you should know four things:

1. I like Mr. Murphy. He's the only teacher I have at OG who doesn't see me for me.

2. Mr. Murphy lives for introductions.

3. The guy from the yearbook line, the one who might have been Danny, has, in fact, turned out to be Danny.

4. If my life were turned into a Shakespearean play, it would be performed as a tragedy.

"Danny," Mr. Murphy continues informatively, "transferred here from Austin, Texas, last year and seems to have fallen behind. That's where you come in." Mr. Murphy gently touches my shoulder. "We need to get Danny back on track, so I'd like for you to visit with him for an hour each week until the end of the grading period. How does that sound?"

"Fine," I mutter, because what else can I say or do? I mean, I want to point my finger at Danny and screech, "You smiled at me! I know you did!" But I'm pretty sure that if I did that, both Mr. Murphy and Danny would think that I'm crazy (which I might just be), so I tuck my hands into my pockets instead.

"Good." Mr. Murphy rocks back and forth on his heels, and I can tell he's pondering his next words. "Danny . . ." He turns to Danny with a nod of his head and says seriously, "I trust you will approach your time with Susie with the same care that you approach the soccer season."

"I promise," Danny says solemnly, nodding back at Mr. Murphy.

"Good. Why don't you two take the first fifteen minutes to get to know each other?" He adjusts his pink tie so that it lies neatly against his charcoal-gray shirt. "Friendship is an essential part of the tutoring process. I'll be next door if you need me." He clicks his tongue. "Carry on."

Without Mr. Murphy, there isn't much for us to do except talk to each other, which is the last thing that I want to do. So, I stare down at the puke-brown carpet instead. I count the pieces of flattened gum. I become one with the carpet fiber. Basically, I try to disappear.

It isn't working. Which is ironic. When you think about it.

"So . . ." Danny says after a while; his hands are also buried deep in his pockets. "You're the girl from the yearbook line. You're"—he pauses to look me directly in the eyes—"the girl who can't smile."

It takes time for the words to even register. Then, it takes even more time for me to understand that he can be so mean. Then, it takes another full minute to get over the sting before I lamely respond, "I *can* smile." Which *is* actually true. I can smile. Sometimes. When I'm alone with Marisol. I can . . .

"I'm not saying you *can't* smile." He shrugs his shoulders, so that his Abercrombie shirt rides up, and I glimpse a sliver of his milk-chocolate abdomen. "I'm just saying that today in the yearbook line you were the girl who, you know, *couldn't*"—he points at his mouth and his smooth pink lips—"smile."

"*But*," I say with a lot more force, because I'm not sure what he expects to get out of this conversation, "I *can* smile."

"*Okay* . . . " His face changes a bit, and I can tell that he's getting my point. "So . . ." He bites his lower lip. "What grade are you in?"

I don't answer him. What's the point? We're never going to be friends. Isn't it obvious?

"Well?" he says, but I stare at him blankly. "Well?"

"Tenth," I mutter.

"So you're like one of those smart people. You're, like, in honors, right?"

"AP. But I'm not that smart," which is a bold-faced lie. Pretty much anyone in advanced-placement classes is really smart, but that's not my fault.

"Well, you must be sort of smart, or why else would Mr. Murphy ask you to tutor me?" Danny raises his eyebrows, and a half smile flutters across his lips. It's like seeing half of the smile he gave me in the yearbook line, and I get a flashback of me standing there, staring at him with my arms hanging limply at my sides. My face turns red, so when Danny asks what period I have Mr. Murphy, I can't help but bark, "Isn't that enough of us trying to be friends?"

The question makes Danny jump back. And instead of feeling just terribly awkward, like I did two minutes ago, I now feel incredibly awkward and stupid.

"Um . . ." Danny taps the palm of his hand against his thigh and gives me a quizzical look. "I mean, I guess so. Yeah."

It takes a few seconds for both of us to recover, but eventually we sit opposite each other at the nearest desks. I do my best to calm myself while I ruffle through my book bag. When I feel slightly okay, I pull out a notebook and write his name across the top of a clean page.

"Why don't you tell me what books you're reading in class and what papers you have due in the next couple of weeks, and then we can go from there." I try to imitate my dad's professor-voice because my own voice seems to be scaring Danny right now.

"You're really organized. Aren't you?" Danny taps his pencil against my notebook. I nod my head. "Do you want to see my syllabus?" he asks, playing with a hangnail on his ring finger.

Again, I nod and he hands me a stained sheet of paper. Then we sit until the silence becomes so thick and gooey that I force myself to say, "You have a paper due in two weeks, right?"

"Yep." He taps his fingers on the desk. "It's on *The Scarlet Letter*."

"Have you finished reading it?"

"Nope." He circles his foot repeatedly.

"Have you even started reading it?"

"Not so much," he mumbles, and his foot jumps to warp speed.

"Look"—my own voice comes back and it's slippery—"I can't help you if you aren't willing to do the work. I have things that I could be doing, too." I lean back and give him the stare.

"Yeah? Like what?" He stares back.

"Stuff."

"What stuff?" he asks.

"Stuff," I repeat firmly.

"Like . . . ?"

"Can we just focus on you?" I ask.

He leans forward and rests his head on his forearms. For a second, I think he's about to go to sleep. Then, real lazylike, he asks, "So, what lunch wave do you have?"

"What difference does it make?"

"Just curious." He sits back in his chair, chews on his lower lip.

"Just read the book, okay?" I'm not going to reveal that Marisol and I practically take lunch in another country. That's none of his business.

"You don't want to tell me about it before I start reading?" Danny asks, which is when I realize that he's looking at me like I'm his own personal set of CliffsNotes.

"*What?*" Does he seriously think that just because I AM a nerd, a geek—whatever he wants to think about me—that I'm going to sit here and summarize the book for him like he's in first grade? "I—I—I . . ." I'm so mad, I'm stuttering. "You—you promised Mr. Murphy. I can't believe you haven't even begun to read the book!"

I start to gather my things.

Danny looks at the clock on the wall and then back to me. "Hey, it's only been twenty minutes!"

"And?" I stuff my notebook into my book bag and give the zipper a harsh tug.

"Hey—" Danny says again, but I'm already at the door. "I didn't say I haven't read it. I've read the first three chapters," he mutters, flipping through the pages.

I turn back to the door. I pull it open.

"Hey," this time his voice is pleading, and even though I know I shouldn't, I can't help myself, I look back. "You'll be back next week, right?" he asks. I shrug my shoulders because I don't know what I'd say if I actually opened my mouth to speak.

"Are you always this tough?" he asks with a crooked smile.

"Maybe," I say. But the truth is I'm not.

# a quick f.y.i.

● ● ●

**the short list:**

1. I don't have a boyfriend.

2. I don't have any friends beside Marisol.

3. When I grow up, I want to be a songwriter.

4. Marisol thinks that I'm obsessed with my mental health.

5. To date, I've had sixteen panic attacks.

6. My father says that I've had none.

7. My grandmother is so completely senile, she pins wads of toilet paper to the crotch of her underwear.

8. My mother died in a car accident when I was nine.

9. Whenever I smell Caress body wash, I think about her.

The long list:

1. I love learning. I hate school. I live for summer breaks. It's about sixty days, during which time I do the following:
   a. Days 1–10: Delete the noise in my head *(Move, bitch; God, you are weird; I'm saving this seat, and that one. Yeah, that one, too.)*
   b. Days 11–40: Exist in a nontoxic, semicomatose state.
   c. Days 41–60: Let Marisol ply her usual tactics of manipulation and lies to persuade me to return to school. *(Nice people do live in this world, and once we graduate we will actually meet these people; Geek is a word to describe people so intellectually and emotionally advanced that civilization often misunderstands them, therefore, the term is a compliment;* and my personal favorite: *people who are assholes are only assholes because they secretly hate themselves so they want to make you hate yourself, too—and because of this reasoning, you should just ignore them anyway.)*

2. I love Marisol. Is it gay to say that? Well, if it is, I'm going to go out on a limb and be heterosexually gay because I really do love her. Marisol makes me feel safe. She never gets frazzled. She's totally solid. I cry . . . well, let's just say that still waters run deep—like oceanic deep.

3. I am not being "self-conscious": People have been saying that I was odd-looking since I was a little girl. Everyone still says it. Some are nice enough to say it behind my back. Others say it by my back, by my locker, on my locker with a red permanent marker that says OWL-GIRL and WHOOOOO. Sometimes . . . they say it to my face.

## FOUR

# helping danny

• • •

on friday, i browbeat myself into talking to mr. murphy after English class. It takes eight students cutting in front of me, plus seven *um*s and sighs, before I'm able to form one complete sentence.

"Um . . . Mr. Murphy?" I say.

"Yes, Susie?" Mr. Murphy beams at me for no other reason than that's how he is. "What can I do for you? I know this assignment hasn't confused you, too."

"No . . . um, the assignment's fine. I mean, it's great. You know I love Jane Austen. Um . . ." I clear my throat. "Really, I don't have a problem with the assignment."

"Good. I'm glad to hear that. Is there another reason you waited to speak with me?"

"Um . . . yeah. I wanted to . . . talk to you . . . about, about . . . Um. I wanted to talk to you about—"

"Danny Diaz?" Mr. Murphy interjects. He leans forward and gives me a concerned look.

"Yeah. Um . . . did Danny say something to you?"

It took days of internal warfare to psych myself up enough to speak to Mr. Murphy about this whole Danny situation. I never thought Danny would beat me to the punch.

"Well, Danny did mention that he was quite unprepared for your first session and that you were understandably upset. He assured me that he would not let you down a second time."

So what? Danny was trying to play Mr. Murphy, too?

"The thing is, Mr. Murphy"—I pause to take a breath—"I don't think I'm the right person to . . . help Danny."

"Oh," Mr. Murphy seems surprised, which surprises me because you would think he saw this coming. "Why is that?"

"Well . . ." The thing is when I practiced my speech—my "I'm quitting tutoring Danny Diaz" speech—I never considered that Mr. Murphy might turn it into a conversation. I thought I'd just quit and be done with it.

"Um . . ." The first step is to stall for time. "Um . . ." The second step is to repeat the first step. And the third step? Lie. "Well, I . . . think that Danny . . . might be more comfortable with someone . . . in his own grade."

"Is that what he told you?" Mr. Murphy asks. He takes his glasses off and wipes them clean with his handkerchief.

"No . . . not in so many words. But he hinted at it." Didn't he?

"Well, Susie"—Mr. Murphy slides his glasses back into place—"I'll definitely speak to Danny about his prejudice toward younger tutors, but I still believe that you are the best person for the job."

"But Mr. Murphy," I protest, "I don't want Danny to feel uncomfortable. Can't he get another tutor? How about Tamara Cruz? She's a tutor, isn't she?"

"Susie," Mr. Murphy says patiently, "Tamara's a sophomore, too. And if she were a junior, I would still say no because I believe that you are the right tutor for Danny. Is there something you're not telling me? Some legitimate reason why you can't tutor him?"

"Um . . ." And here's where I start to consider the unthinkable. I start to think that my only way out of this terrible situation is to tattle on Danny. So I take a deep breath to prepare myself because if that's what I have to do, that's what I'll do.

"Look, Mr. Murphy, the truth is . . . The truth"—I clear my throat—"The truth is . . . I'm nervous that I'm going to do a bad job and he'll fail."

I guess I am a lot of things, just not a tattletale.

"Susie," Mr. Murphy says, "you're just going to have to trust me on this. I know you're the right tutor for Danny. I believe this. And I believe in you. Will you trust me?" He smiles, that wonderfully open smile of his.

"Yes, Mr. Murphy." My shoulders slump in defeat.

"Good." He rises from his desk and pulls out a piece of paper with a tiny doodle in the corner. "Now, I'm glad you stayed after. I wanted to talk to you about your Jane Austen paper. Absolutely brilliant. How do you do it?" he asks, with a wink.

"I don't know, Mr. Murphy." I let out a sigh. "I just do."

# my m.i.a. d.a.d.

● ● ●

a week later around midnight, my dad and i cross paths in the kitchen.

"How's school?" he asks, his face buried halfway in the refrigerator.

"Okay. I'm studying for a trig test."

Even though my dad and I have shared space for fifteen years, I'm always unsure how to begin conversations with him. I guess it's because I haven't had enough practice.

"How's it going over there?" I nod toward the study, my dad's home away from home. He spends like 90 percent of his time there, when he isn't teaching lit classes at the University of Miami.

He shrugs his shoulders. His eyes are red and droopy.

"How's Grandma?" I ask, partially because I want to know, partially because I can't think of anything else to say.

"Still forgetful." He grabs a water bottle from the fridge. "Dad's taking her to see a specialist on Friday. Hopefully, the doctor will be able to give us some answers." He shifts uncomfortably on his heels. "Well, I should get back."

"Yeah." I grab an apple from the fruit basket. "Me, too."

And just like that, we go our separate ways.

during the year that i was ten, i used to crawl into my dad's bed, because I was too scared to sleep alone. And no matter what time of night it was, I always found him doing the same thing—lying quietly on my mother's side of the bed, his head turned into her pillow.

At first, I tried to get him to notice me. I'd call out his name from the doorway, but then I realized that it didn't matter if I was there, because he couldn't see me, not really. So I climbed up on the bed, too, and pushed myself against him so that I could feel the heat from his skin. I lay as still as possible next to him. I rested my head on her pillow. I closed my eyes and imagined that the breathing that I heard next to me—my father's breathing—was her breathing.

Each night, I pretended. And slowly, very slowly, I learned to sleep again. But not my father. He never slept. Not in that room, maybe not in any room of the house. He never slept. And I wondered if it was because he didn't know my trick. I wondered if I should have taught him to pretend.

# SIX

# two wednesdays later

...

two wednesdays later, i wait for danny in the library. we're meeting for our third weekly tutorial, and he's late. Thirty minutes late to be exact. Which is so unsurprising that . . . I'm annoyed at myself for being surprised.

It's not like he's responsible. I mean, responsible students don't get behind in their classes. Right? Responsible students don't need tutors. Responsible students don't make me wait. ALONE. At school. It's like having someone stamp LOSER in bright red ink on my forehead. Not that I need the stamp.

Where is he? I prop my head up with my fist and write out a list of places where he might possibly be. I come up with the following:

1. He's decided that he doesn't need me anymore to pass his midterm, so he's blowing me off without even saying why.

2. He's a jerk, just like I thought he was, and he's totally taking advantage of me and my time.

3. He's outside buying me a pack of Combos because he knows
   how much I love them.

The third thought unexpectedly pops into my head. I erase it immediately.

"Wait long?" I smell the stench of sweat and muddy grass long
before I hear Danny's voice.

"You are"—I consult my watch again to gauge the exact extent of
his tardiness—"thirty-five, no, make that thirty-six minutes late."

"Oops." Danny shrugs his shoulders and smiles, as if dimples
were meant to stand in for all apologies.

"Oops?" I repeat.

"I must have lost track of time. I just got out of practice."

"I can tell." I lower my eyes back to my textbook. "I can smell
you."

"Huh?" he says uncertainly.

"Look at you." I point to his sweat-soaked body and greasy,
Combo-less hands.

He glances down at his uniform. It clings to him. "A water pipe
broke, so the showers were closed. Do I really smell that bad?" He
takes a whiff of his armpit and bursts out laughing. "Okay . . . if the
rest of me smells like that, you're in trouble."

"You couldn't smell yourself before you walked in?" I cover my
nose with my hand.

"No . . ." He plops into the seat across from me with a loud *thud*.
"Stop all the drama."

"I'm not being dramatic. Okay? Just open your book. Okay?" I
reach for my notebook and turn the page. I head it the same way I have
for the last three sessions: DANNY DIAZ in capital letters. Underneath I write: *The Scarlet Letter*. Then I wait patiently (or impatiently, if
you count my several sighs of aggravation) for him to locate his book.

"Crap. I think I left my book in my locker."

"You left your book in your locker?"

It was one thing to show up late, but he had to show up late AND stinky AND unapologetic AND unprepared.

"I'm sorry," he says, dumping the entire contents of his backpack onto the library table. "I thought I grabbed it before practice."

"You thought you grabbed it before practice?"

"Yeah." He tosses aside his cleats and rummages through fifty loose papers. "I don't have it."

"But you had your soccer clothes. Your"—I push the offensive cleats away—"cleats."

"Yeah, and?"

"So you were prepared for soccer, just not prepared for me?"

"What's your deal?" he snaps.

"My deal?" I repeat, feeling an inexplicable amount of frustration.

"Yeah," he says, glaring at me. "YOUR DEAL."

"My deal," my voice rises impatiently, "is . . . YOU . . ."

And this is where I stop talking. I stop talking because I want to say, *You aren't even sorry. You aren't taking my time seriously. You don't care that I've been sitting here like an idiot for the last thirty minutes, while everyone around me thinks that I'm a loser because I'm here— alone.*

But I can't say that, can I?

So when I start again, I say, or rather I yell, "You STINK!" which makes every single person in the library turn around and stare at ME.

Danny is also staring at me. "You're so loud," he whispers with a smile.

"And you're so stupid," I whisper back while I gather my things.

"You're kidding? You're leaving again?"

"You," I force myself to lean forward, "really stink . . . and you were late and unprepared. I can't tutor under these circumstances."

"'I can't tutor under these circumstances,'" he repeats after me.

"Don't mock me," I hiss.

"'Don't mock me,'" he says in a high-pitched, whiny voice.

"I don't sound like that," I say hotly.

"Yes, you do." He raises an eyebrow at me.

"Screw you," I burst out.

"Oh, okay . . ."

His tone is playful, but I don't care. I want to slap him.

"Well . . . ?" He's laughing openly now.

"Well, what?" I narrow my eyes until I can barely see. Why don't I just walk away?

"Are you or are you not going to—"

"Just shut up!"

"You shut up," Danny whispers, "The librarian is comin—"

And that's when it happens—my first outward moment of temporary insanity. I don't realize I've tossed a hardcover dictionary at him until I see the book flying in slow motion across the top of his head. All I feel is the adrenaline that saturates my brain and encourages me to lean forward to maliciously whisper, "You stink," before I stalk past the reprimanding librarian and out the green double doors.


"i can't believe that you tossed the dictionary at him."

That night, I call Marisol and give her a play-by-play.

"I know! I know!" I screech. I've never been so brazen in my life. I am, without a doubt, high on the rush. "I was insane. I was like, 'Pick your mouth up off the floor, asshole.'"

"You called him an asshole?"

"No, but I thought it." Actually, I didn't think it, but it just makes my story sound that much cooler.

"You're crazy," Marisol laughs. "Do you think he'll say something to you tomorrow?"

"Oh, crap." I hadn't even thought about tomorrow. To be honest, I hadn't thought past my conversation with Marisol.

"Well, don't freak out. He can't fight you. He's a guy."

Well, duh . . . guys don't fight girls. Do they? Last year Piper Blythe got into a fight with a guy. He called her a bitch for cutting the lunch line. She called him an asshole for calling her a bitch. He said if the name fits. She tossed her milk at him and the next thing you knew, they were fighting.

"What if he tries to fight me?" I ask Marisol.

"Danny? No way," Marisol chuckles. "At worst, he'll get Dalia to knock you out."

"Thanks," I say sourly.

We're quiet for a couple of minutes. Without the hum of the phone, I'd have no clue that we were still connected.

"Marisol?"

"Sorry, I'm having a *Gilmore Girls* marathon. My mom just bought me all seven seasons on DVD. Hey, does Lorelai ever get with—" Her voice cuts out like she has another call, which is strange because she has her own phone line and, as far as I know, I'm the only person besides her dad who has her number. And her dad never calls.

"Do you have another call?"

"No," she says, sounding distracted, "my phone's . . . dying. I . . . um . . . have to recharge. I'll see you tomorrow, okay? Bye."

"Yeah," I say to the sudden disconnection.

And then I wonder: when did Marisol get a cordless?

after i hang up with marisol, i'm conflicted. will danny confront me? He doesn't seem the type, but then anything is possible—just ask Piper. Should I apologize to him? No way. He's completely obnoxious.

I dig out my trig book, and this time I try in earnest to study. But I find myself doodling—asteroids falling to earth and little punk girls with heads that explode. It doesn't take a rocket scientist to figure out that my subconscious is speaking out.

I toss my book onto the floor and roll onto my back. I really should tidy up my bedroom. It's piggish.

*"Are you organized?"* Danny's question pops into my head.

*"Always."*

Yep, I'm a big pretender.

I'm too nervous to clean, so I pick up my guitar and begin to strum it. I mouth the words to a song that I'm working on. It goes something like this:

*I see you walking down the street*
*You're looking kind of sweet*
*I'm wondering if you'll smile at me and if we'll ever meet*
*Today's the day I'd like to smile and say hello boy*
*But there's one thing that you really, really need to know*

And that's about as far as I get. I play a little longer, but I can't think of anything else. The only thing I can think of is Danny. Why does he keep creeping into my head?

I put my guitar away in utter frustration and turn out my bedroom light.

And that's exactly how my dad finds me—curled under my covers, sighing so exceptionally loud that for once he can't avoid me.

"Everything okay?" He stands awkwardly at the end of my bed and gives one of my curls a light tug.

"Stop." I move my head out of reach.

"How's school?" he asks

"Fine. Work?" I counter.

He tries to stifle a yawn.

"You know, sleep is actually a good thing," I tell him.

"I will. Soon." He smiles, but the smile seems worn. "How was school today? How was tutoring?"

"Well, actually today I had . . ." I start, but then I glance up and find him staring absently at the goldfish alarm clock perched on my nightstand table. "A great day," I finish with as much enthusiasm as I can muster.

"Sounds like you have everything under control," he says.

"Yeah." I look at his saggy face. I remind myself that I should feel sorry for him. He's Mr. Robotic. He doesn't need food. He doesn't need conversation. He doesn't need anything, not even me.

"Dad?" I pull him down onto my bed and rest my head on his lap. I keep his hand in my hand. I watch him, the lines that have settled like canyons across his face. It's so rare for him to be near me—so rare for him to touch me. It's like he's slipping away.

"Yes?" His breath smells nice, like mint Listerine. I inhale deeply.

"Do you think we could spend this Saturday together?"

He tries to pull his hand away, but I hold on. "Susie, you know I'm on a deadline. I'm almost done, but until then, I really should buckle down and finish the manuscript."

"Okay." I mask the disappointment in my voice. I let his hand go and it hovers above my ear. "Well, maybe then?"

I wait for him to answer, to make a commitment to me, knowing that just like his hand hovers above my ear, the words that I want to hear are there, hovering on his lips.

But the words don't come. And maybe it's selfish of me to want to hear them, but I do. So I lie as still as I can and I hope. Even as he presses his lips against my cheek and shuts my door, I hope.

# SEVEN

# tamara

• • •

in driver's ed, there are six people to every squad, and although the coach swears that the squads were chosen randomly, I think there must have been some divine intervention at work because about two-thirds of my squad is of equal social and intellectual atomic structure. But there are differences, too. My squad consists of:

1. Tamara—Sophomore class president.

2. Bobby—Co-captain of the junior varsity bowling team.

3. Luis—The other co-captain of the junior varsity bowling team.

4. Jessica—Junior varsity cheerleader. Popular, pretty, and smart. (You know I hate her.)

5. José—Not mainstream popular but well liked among the burnout crowd. (My guess is that it's not really hard to find friends if you've got some pot to share.)

6. Me—Party of one.

In this group I do okay. I guess you could say that besides Jessica, everyone's nice. That's really more than I had hoped for.

Right now, I'm waiting for my turn to park in reverse and spending every second of it hoping that José, our assigned squad captain, will get me through the experience. See, José's like a driver's ed superstar. He can change lanes, parallel park, stop on a dime—whatever. Our driver's ed coach eats him up—red eyes and all—because there's no limit to his driving ability.

After José finishes, Jessica slides into the driver's seat and takes off with a screech. She's a crazy driver, and I don't know how she got to be co-captain, but I bet it has something to do with her teeny-tiny skirts, minuscule thighs, and glossy black hair.

"You look worried." Every now and then Tamara likes to take time from writing in her student government notebook to talk to me.

"A little," I admit. Jessica skids to a stop. From across the lot, the coach shoots her a thumbs-up.

"Yeah, me, too," Tamara says. And I'm taken aback because in the ten years that I've known Tamara, I've never once heard her admit to being nervous.

"You're nervous?"

"Yeah, I don't know what it is, but I just can't operate in reverse. I get all discombobulated. Ya know?" She shakes her head.

I sigh in agreement.

"So," she says. "I hear you're tutoring Danny Diaz."

"Who told you?" It's not like I've told anyone besides Marisol. And I can't imagine that Danny Diaz feels the need to broadcast his academic ineptitude to anyone.

"Oh, you know, somebody . . ."

Somebody, I wonder. Or half the library?

"So . . ." Tamara smiles, and I notice what straight, white teeth she has. Tamara isn't conventionally pretty, but when she smiles or talks about things that are interesting to her, you just can't help but get sucked in. I guess that makes her an unusually attractive person. "Do you know if he has a girlfriend?" she asks rather lightly.

"What?" I didn't even know that she knew Danny, let alone liked him.

"Well . . . ?" Tamara flashes me her *aren't I brilliant* smile.

"I don't know. We don't talk about anything besides English." And barely that. With three meetings behind us (two of them filled with my emotional instability), Danny and I had barely had time to discuss *The Scarlet Letter*, let alone his relationship status.

"Hey"—she cocks her head to the side—"do you think you could ask? If you don't mind . . ." Again, she smiles.

"Well, I don't really think that would be appropriate. You know," I explain lamely, "a violation of the student/tutor relationship."

"Yeah, that's true, but . . . it's not like you're getting paid. I mean the position is totally volunteer, right? And asking personal questions is how you get to know someone better, which is important to a working relationship." Tamara closes the deal like a true politician.

I paste on a stiff smile and debate whether I feel queasy because Jessica has just thrown the car into park or because the idea of Danny with thousand-watt Tamara is nauseating?

"Susie," José screams, his body halfway out the car window, "you're holding up the line!"

*Which seems to always be my problem*, I think. "I have to go." I leap to my feet and take five grateful steps forward before Tamara calls out to me.

"Susie," she says, "please."

It's sad, really, because that's all it takes. One simple *please* and I freeze.

"Please," she repeats again.

I crumble. "Fine, I'll see what I can do."

"Oh!" Tamara rushes forward and gives me a forceful hug. "Thanks, like a million times. I mean it."

"You're welcome," I say. And despite myself, I can't believe how nice it feels to hear those words—*thanks* and *please*—from someone other than Marisol. It's like—

"Susie, c'mon!" Jose waves me in like an air traffic controller.

It's like . . . driving in reverse with your eyes closed.

# EIGHT

# just maybe . . . a connection

• • •

after failing my driver's ed exam, getting a c on my trig test, and debating for the thousandth time whether Tamara and Danny might possibly have a future together, I come to one and only one conclusion: I never want to leave my bed. Ever.

That is, until my dad decides to attack my bedroom door with the raw force of his writer's knuckles. Then, I want to get out of bed for the sole purpose of killing.

"Come on, Susie." My dad says, followed by two sharp raps on the buckling pressboard. "Susie, get up."

Question: if your daughter's light is out, her door is closed, and other than for the fart that she let rip (and I mean rip) half an hour ago, you haven't heard a peep out of her for the LAST FIVE HOURS, what do you think she might be doing?

Answer: SLEEPING. I'M SLEEPING.

Isn't it obvious?

"Susie?" There is a knuckle scrape, followed by an irritating *pound, pound.*

Apparently not.

"Dad," I moan, "I'm tired!"

"Susie," my dad growls, "I'm on a call. You have a visitor." His tone is short, which is surprising because I never knew that automatic-pilot dads come preprogrammed with two settings.

"Fine." I fight to focus on the light slipping underneath the cracks of my bedroom door. "I'm awake."

"Good." I hear him retreat down the hall to the study.

I glance at Mr. Swims-A-Lot, the neon-green goldfish clock that my mom bought me for my ninth birthday. It's eight forty-five p.m. School ended at two-thirty, and only now is Marisol responding to my S.O.S. cry for help (one e-mail, two voice mails, and a dire hand-written note scribbled in purple highlighter).

"Marisol," I mutter, stopping at my father's study to listen to his important phone call.

"Yeah," I hear him murmur. "Uh-huh. That's a very good idea. I understand, Leslie."

His important phone call is Leslie? Marisol's mom, Leslie?

"Marisol," I say, popping a breath mint into my mouth as I walk through our U-shaped house and step around the corner of the family room and into the foyer, "why is your mom talking to my dad on the pho—"

"It's not Marisol."

The sight of Danny Diaz standing in my foyer, coupled with the overwhelming smell of his cologne, stops me from talking, walking, or doing anything else.

"Danny?" I step back into a bookcase. "What are you doing here? I rub my eyes roughly, believing that if I rub hard enough he'll disappear. "How do you know where I live?"

"Tamara," he says simply.

"Tamara?"

"Tamara, um, Cruz. We have sixth period SAT prep together . . ."

I give him a blank look so he continues.

"You used to ride the same private bus in junior high. . . . Her dad teaches at UM with your dad. . . . You have the same—"

"Driver's ed class together. Yeah . . . I know." But how did he know? Was he talking to Tamara about me?

"I asked her where you live because I wanted to come here. I wanted to talk to you."

I move slowly toward the living room sofa, keeping my eyes on him at all times. The ceiling fan whirls above us, spreading the aroma of Danny everywhere and filling my ears with a buzzing noise. I shiver. My pajamas—a pair of boxers and a white wifebeater, sans bra—suddenly seem transparent. It's like I'm standing naked in front of Danny. I burrow my body into the corner of the sofa, hiding my chest behind an oversized throw pillow.

"You asked Tamara where I live?" I clarify. Danny nods his head, a hesitant smile threatening the corners of his lips. "But why?" I ask, which is a good question. *Why?*

"Um . . ." Danny sits opposite me on the love seat. "I wanted to . . . um . . . you . . ." He stops abruptly and rubs the side of his mouth. "You've got some . . ."

"What?" I stare at him blankly.

He rubs the side of his mouth again, shakes his head, and licks his thumb. He leans forward, cups my chin, and rubs his thumb lightly over my skin.

"Drool," he says, chuckling.

Ten thousand butterflies. When Danny's finger connects with my chin, ten thousand butterflies explode in my belly. I mean, here he is: Danny, with his face six inches from mine, and all I can wonder is: is my breath mint working?

"You came here to wipe drool from my cheek?" I try hard to speak without opening my mouth.

"No." He leans back and looks at me with those penny eyes.

"I came to say that I'm sorry for the other day. For the library."

"Oh . . . oh . . ." My eyes pop open and I can practically feel the eye crud falling out. "That's why you're here? Now. In my house? Here." I'd keep rambling till the end of time, but something, somewhere deep inside me tells me to shut up.

"Yeah," he says, shaking his head.

So this is it? I feel relieved, and I feel something else. Let down? Disappointed?

"It's just that sometimes I say what I'm thinking but I don't think. I just open my mouth and, you know, speak."

"Sure." I shrug my shoulders.

"I'm not trying to be . . ." His voice trails off.

How could I have ever thought he could hit me?

"Sometimes, I just talk and stupid things happen. Like yesterday, I was telling Dalia about the library—"

"You told your sister about yesterday?" My heart pops like a firecracker. The catch. This was the catch. Danny Diaz would never hit a girl. He has his sister for that.

"Well"—he takes off his baseball cap—"it was kind of hard to hide this at the dinner table." He leans forward to show me the quarter-sized knot on the top of his head.

"Dinner?" I say. "Like with the entire family?"

"Yeah . . ." Danny gives me a strange look.

Question: is it more shocking to find out that you've maimed one of the hottest boys in your school? Or that the hot boy sits down to have dinner with his family?

Answer: I wasn't sure.

"Wow. I did that." Without thinking, I touch the knot and feel terribly guilty (and slightly satisfied) when Danny flinches.

"Yeah, did you have to choose the unabridged dictionary? Couldn't you just have used your pocket Webster?"

"Ah, you're a funny guy," I whisper.

"Is this supposed to be funny?" Danny reenacts the hit in slow motion. I can't help but laugh.

"I guess so." His dimples appear. I want to rub my finger in the indent.

"You're lucky. I actually considered using the *Encyclopedia Britannica*." I pause. "Letters A–G."

He runs his hand protectively over his skull. "That would have hurt."

"What did you tell your sister?" I am curious. I've never had my name pass between the lips of the socially elite.

"I told her about what happened. What you said, and what I said, and well"—Danny looks down at his hands before speaking—"I don't know. I just told her some stuff."

"Oh."

"So why did you throw the book at me?"

Good question. Too bad I didn't have one good, rational answer to give to him.

"I don't know. You really smelled, and you were mimicking me, and you were there with this *I don't care that I'm late* attitude. I just wanted to . . ." I trail off. It's obvious from the knot on his head what I wanted to do.

"Well, I couldn't help stinking. The showers really weren't working. And being late . . . sometimes the coach keeps us late. And, I was a jerk mimicking you like that, but I was just playing."

At this point, he could tell me that he likes green eggs and ham. I don't care. I'm stuck somewhere between understanding that our knees are touching and that he, too, washes his face with Neutrogena. I can smell it on him.

"So . . ." he says.

"So . . ."

"I'm sorry." He looks me straight in the eye. "I'm going to try to do better. I'm going to try to be prepared and not stink."

"I'm sorry, too," I mutter, looking away.

"What?" He leans in closer.

"I'm sorry," I repeat in a clearer yet equally low tone.

"Hey, no problem. Just, if you don't mind, stand over there," he points at the wall and grabs a book off the coffee table, "while I throw this at you."

I smile and he smiles back—penny eyes, dimple indents, bright white teeth and all. He smiles back, and I feel ridiculous because never, in my entire life, has it felt so good to see someone smile.

Which might explain why I suddenly blurt out, "Do you have a girlfriend?"

He tilts his head to the side and considers me. Even though I am holding my breath, I tell myself that I really am asking this question for Tamara.

"No. Why?" His eyes seem to challenge me to admit that I like him.

"Um . . ." *Tell the truth*, something deep inside whispers. "Um, because Tamara wants to know." I regret the words as soon as they leave my mouth. Why did I just point out that Tamara likes him? Who wouldn't like thousand-watt Tamara over ten-watt me?

"Tamara?" He doesn't seem surprised. "So, we're cool?"

"We're cool," I reply, watching him walk to the door.

"So, I'll see you in school tomorrow?" His hand pauses on the doorknob.

"Yeah."

"Cool."

"Cool," I repeat.

After he leaves, I flick off the living room light and sit in the dark. I watch the shadows dance as random car lights flood the room. In the dark, everything changes. Just like me.

# NINE

# lots and lots of candy

• • •

"how do i look?"

Marisol's mom, Leslie, is a psychologist, and she's usually 100 percent confident, except for tonight. Tonight, she keeps asking how she looks. It's really annoying because the whole conversation sound like listening to a CD for the millionth time. It's like this:

MARISOL: Mom, you look great.

Time passes.

MARISOL: Seriously, Mom, you look perfect.

Time passes.

MARISOL (with a really bad French accent): Mom, you are *tres fabulous*.

And it's true, Marisol's mom does look fabulous.

Tonight is Halloween. The night that Marisol and I rent all the Halloween movies from the video store, curl up on the family room sofa, and eat all the candy that we're supposed to be passing out to the neighborhood kids.

Even without all the candy (okay, slight exaggeration), I'd still have fun on Halloween. Marisol and I dress up every year. Last year, we were the two crotchety old men from *Waiting for Godot*. This year, we're paying homage to Lewis Carroll. I'm Alice and Marisol's the Mad Hatter. Very appropriate, I told her.

"Do you think this outfit is too skimpy?" Leslie asks, indicating that we've moved on to the second phase of the evening: The *am I a slut or what?* portion.

Ever since Marisol's parents got divorced, Leslie has spent Halloween night worrying that she looks slutty, which would be equivalent to calling an Amish girl a whore.

See, Leslie's super-big on respecting yourself and your body. That's not to say that she doesn't make the most of her assets. The woman has buns of steel. She runs every day and takes spinning classes three times a week. She says exercise and shopping are her forms of therapy. She keeps inviting me and Marisol to speed-walk at the mall. Me? Speed-walk at the mall? As if. But Marisol . . . well, Marisol is on the fast track to becoming a junior shopaholic. And her butt looks pretty tight, too.

"Well?" Leslie takes another spin in front of us, and both Marisol and I try not to giggle. Last year, Marisol's mom was a cop, and this year, she's a construction worker. Both outfits were tremendously skanky before Leslie spent twelve hours modifying them. Now they were absolutely puritanical.

"Mom, please." Marisol pops open the first three buttons of Leslie's blouse. "They're just breasts. Let them breathe."

"I don't know . . . Susie?"

"You look great."

"Yeah? Thanks. I wonder what your father will wear."

Which shows how little Leslie knows about my father. "He'll wear Dockers and a polo shirt."

"Dockers and a polo shirt? You think?" Leslie asks no one in particular.

Leslie invited my father to her friend's annual Halloween party because (as Marisol put it) she's concerned that my dad spends way too much time alone (i.e., he's about to crack up and shouldn't we pull an intervention?). Whatever. Anyway, the real surprise was that Daddy Dearest said yes.

That's right. Yes.

I'm assuming that this is his way of thanking Leslie for helping him research his latest novel. It's a psychological thriller about blah, blah, blah. (Okay, I never really pay attention to what he's writing.) But still, I have to give Leslie props. I can't remember the last time my dad went out, even with me.

"You told your dad to be here at seven, right?" Leslie asks for the twentieth time.

"Uh-huh." Actually, I told my father seven fifteen because Leslie is notorious for being late, and my father is notorious for being overly punctual. I figured if I fudged the numbers, the imbalance of their two personalities would even things out. Clearly, I was wrong. It's now seven thirty, and Leslie's still standing by the window hoping to spot him.

"Do you think I should call? Oh, wait. There he is."

I glance out the window, and sure enough there's dear old Dad dressed in beige Dockers and a white polo shirt with a sheepish grin on his face.

"Sorry." My father apologizes when I greet him outside. "I lost track of time . . . writing."

"Uh-huh. Is that for me?" I grab for the Godiva bag he's clutching to his chest like a safety blanket.

"Actually"—he deflects my hands and plants an awkward kiss on my cheek—"I had trouble deciding what to wear. Leslie said to wear a construction hat and faded jeans, but I don't own faded jeans."

"But you own a construction hat?"

"Anyway, I'm a college professor." He points to a pencil tucked behind his ear and a super-tiny edition of *Wuthering Heights* nestled casually in his back pocket. "What do you think?"

"Very original."

"Yeah?" He seems relieved.

"No." I shake my head at him.

"Well." He peers over my shoulder as the door opens behind me. "We're about to find out."

"There you are." Leslie stands behind me and gives my shoulder a light squeeze. "You're normally so punctual. We were starting to get worried."

"I'm sorry—"

"No, don't be." She pinches his arm playfully. "I'm teasing. What do you have there?"

"This"—my dad thrust the Godiva bag at her—"is to thank you for your invitation."

"Oh, no thanks needed," Leslie says, opening the bag. "I'm just so glad you could come. Wow, Godiva." She smiles brightly at him. "Thank you. That's very nice."

"Well." My father clears his throat the way that he always does when he's extremely nervous. "Let's just say that I haven't been invited out in a real long time. Thank you," he finishes quietly.

"I'm glad you could make it, Joe." Leslie touches his hand lightly. "And I like your costume," she says sincerely. "The book is a nice touch."

"Is my mom flirting with your dad?" Marisol whispers to me.

"I don't think so," I whisper back, my stomach suddenly turning. Is Marisol crazy?

"It looks like flirting to me. And I think your dad is flirting back."

"That's not flirting. That's being polite."

"No," Marisol says sweetly, "that's flirting."

I follow Marisol's gaze. What is she seeing that I'm not? Two grown adults can go out to a coed gathering without it meaning SOMETHING. Yeah, sure, my dad was still standing in Marisol's foyer wearing the same sheepish grin he walked in with. And, sure, Leslie's hand was lingering uncomfortably close to my dad's hand so that if they sneezed, they might accidentally touch. But when did that constitute flirting?

OMG, are they flirting?

"Okay, girls." Leslie kisses Marisol gently on the forehead and hugs me tightly. Which totally pisses me off. Not at Leslie, but at Marisol. I mean, how could Marisol imply that her mother—her wonderful mother—might try to steal, I mean flirt with, my dad?

"Okay. Susie"—my dad pats me twice on the back—"be good, and don't eat all the candy."

"I won't," I promise, grabbing him by the collar and unexpectedly digging my face into his shoulder.

"Oh, okay." My dad places two more awkward pats on my back. "Okay."

"Remember, don't let any strangers in the house. Don't open the door for anyone who doesn't have children, and"—Leslie smiles at the both of us—"no boys."

"Okay, Mom." Marisol shoves them toward the door.

"And lock the—"

"Door," Marisol finishes, slamming the door shut. "Finally."

"Finally," I repeat.

"Boys," she says.

"As if."

"So, our parents, huh?"

"Whatever," I mumble, looking out the window. My dad is helping Leslie into the passenger side of his car.

"Let's put in a movie," Marisol yells from the family room.

"Coming," I yell back, but I can't . . . not until they've driven away.

# TEN

# a definite connection

· · ·

"i'm ready to quit."

One hour later, Marisol and I have handed out nearly three-fourths of the candy, and I'm having the time of my life. All the little kids love my costume. They keep calling me Alice and tugging on my blond wig.

"Why?" I'm totally not ready to give up the fun.

"'Cause," Marisol whines. "We're not going to have enough candy for all the movies. And I'm sick of seeing kids that we know from school."

Marisol does have a point there. So far we've seen at least ten kids from OG. Some were actually trick-or-treating, which was ridiculous, so we didn't open the door for them. And others were with a younger sibling. Lisa, a girl from my trig class, showed up with her niece.

"Yeah, well they haven't all been so bad," I say, adjusting my wig. "Lisa was nice. But you are right about the candy. We're running out." No leftover candy was a possibility that I had not considered, and one, I was sure, that I could not live with. "Okay, we'll do just one more."

"You're getting off on this Alice thing, aren't you?"

"Just one more. Think of the kids!" I grab my belly and moan. "Those poor, chocolate-deprived, sugar-starved, middle-class kids."

"You're crazy," Marisol says laughing.

"And you"—I slap her oversized hat off her head—"are mad."

"Funny," Marisol says dryly.

"I do try," I respond as the doorbell rings. "What?"

Marisol is eyeing me most suspiciously, and I know why. For most of the night, we've been arguing over candy distribution. Thanks to quick feet and fast reflexes, I've done 70 percent of the distribution, not that Marisol hasn't put up a fight. She's got a fast right elbow, and during our last encounter I took a blow to my side. I'm still slightly in pain, but when Marisol screams, "Doorbell!" and leaps for the basket of candy on the dining room table, I can't help but spring into action.

"My turn, again," I yell tauntingly, snatching the basket from her hands. She grabs my blond wig and sends me tumbling backward, managing to catch the basket in midair before it hits the floor.

When I finally get the door open, I'm out of breath and holding Marisol at bay with one hand. "Trick or treat," I tell a bouncy strawberry-blond mini-person wrapped in a pink tulle ballerina outfit.

"Trick or treat," Marisol whispers weakly behind me.

"Is that your monster?" I ask the girl, pointing to a six-foot green-eyed monster standing behind her. The little girl nods her head solemnly and then thrusts a plastic pumpkin basket at me.

"Ooh, you remind me of cotton candy," I tell her, and she does. From her pink bun to her pink dance slippers, she seems fluffed up. "You're very bouncy," I tell her, noting the way she hops from side to side. "Good dance moves."

"Let me look," Marisol jumps up and down behind me.

"Are you going to be nice?" I whisper.

"Yes," she answers reluctantly.

"Okay," I open the door wider, and Marisol squishes in beside me.

"What's your name?" I ask the ballerina, kneeling down.

"Lucy."

"How old are you, Lucy?" Marisol asks.

"I'm five." She holds up five fingers with one hand.

"Wow," Marisol says. "You're a big girl. Is that your Daddy?" Marisol asks, pointing to the monster.

"No, that's my cousin."

"Okay, well, do you want to say something?" Marisol prods.

"Uh-uh," Lucy shakes her head eagerly.

"Trick or treat," I whisper as a reminder.

"Trick or treat," Lucy says. "I gotta pee."

"Oh, you're going for a trick," I tell her. "That's clever. Well, here's your treat anyway," I pat her bun. "Should we give one of these to your cousin, Lucy? Would you like one, too?" I ask the silent monster. "That's a good choice," I tell him when he picks the mini Snickers bar.

"I want one, too," Lucy yells. "I gotta pee!" She bounces faster than before and squeezes her legs together.

"That's a funny trick," I tell her, shaking my head at Marisol.

"Why does she keep doing that?" Marisol asks pointing at her.

"I don't know. Are you trying to show us a new dance?" I ask.

"Maybe she's stretching out?" suggests Marisol.

"Or maybe she stepped in an ant pile?" I hypothesize.

"Or maybe," interjects the monster, "she really has to pee."

"Spoilsport," Marisol and I yell at him.

"Do I . . . ?" I stare at the monster. Something in his muffled monster-voice seems oddly familiar.

"Lucy," the monster reprimands, "I told you to go before we left."

"That voice," I whisper to Marisol, "is really familiar."

"I really gotta pee," Lucy says, putting her hands between her legs.

"Can she use the bathroom?" the monster asks.

"Sure—"

"Hold on." Marisol puts her hand out like a crossing guard. "Give us a minute," Marisol says before slamming the door shut. "What if this is a total setup?"

"The girl has to pee," I tell Marisol, trying to pull the door open.

"Don't you think that monster looks suspicious? And if you recognize his voice, maybe he's one of the jerks from school."

I look at the monster through the peephole. He really does look suspicious, but, then again, what monster doesn't? And why do I recognize his voice? I peek out for a second look. Lucy is no longer bouncing frantically, she's crying.

"She's crying," I tell Marisol. "I really think we should let her use the bathroom."

"Man . . ." Marisol shifts indecisively. "Okay."

We open the door. The monster is crouched down next to Lucy, his mask pulled up.

"Isn't that Danny Diaz?" Marisol asks, turning her head sideways.

And it is. It's Danny Diaz, standing in Marisol's doorway in a puddle of pee.

"Wow. Weird," Marisol says.

"Yeah," I say, because what else can I say? What are the chances of this ever happening to anyone else but me? "Weird."


"i really am sorry," danny says apologetically. "that was completely gross."

It's true, something as small as fifteen minutes can really make a difference in your life. Just look at me now. Here I am sitting in Marisol's living room with Danny Diaz staring at me and Marisol kissing a five-year-old's butt in the kitchen. And all of that happened in just fifteen minutes.

And two weeks ago, I was sitting in my living room across from Danny Diaz, having the most intimate conversation of my entire life—and that experience really only lasted like fifteen minutes, too.

And every Wednesday at three thirty, I sit across a library desk and stare at Danny Diaz for an hour. And every fifteen minutes, I can't help thinking, *What if . . . ?*

It's just a weird coincidence, is all I'm saying.

Sprinkles of laughter tumble out of the kitchen, where Marisol and Lucy are playfully fighting over the exact location to wedge a Snickers bar in the enormous ice cream sundae that they've concocted. Guilt always turns Marisol into the ideal host.

"My aunt should be here soon." Danny looks at his watch. His gaze wanders over his shoulder, toward the kitchen. "You think they're okay—alone and stuff?" He looks nervous. I'm pretty sure he's wondering what other accidents Lucy's planning on having tonight.

"Don't worry," I reassure Danny, "Marisol's got her covered. Thank God her old ballet clothes fit Lucy. I can't believe how loud she can scream."

"Yeah, she can be real loud sometimes. It's a Latin thing," he says with a wink.

"Don't let Marisol hear you say that," I tell him. "She's totally against the idea that Hispanics are loud."

"What is she? Cuban American?" he asks.

"Two hundred percent," I tell him.

"Me, too. How about you?" he asks me.

"With a last name like Shannon? *Puh-leeze.*" I give him a look. "I'm a combo—half Irish from my dad's side, half Puerto Rican from my mom's side."

"That's weird," he says. "Shannon, huh? Your dad *is* pale like Casper."

"No, he's not." I toss a throw pillow at him in protest.

"Yeah, he is." Danny grabs the pillow and tosses it back. I duck so that it doesn't hit me. "But"—he leans forward and takes in the features on my face—"you have a little bit of color. You must look more like your—"

"So, do you watch Lucy a lot?" I change the subject quickly.

"Sometimes." Danny gives me an odd look. He glances toward the kitchen. Lucy's is asking Marisol a thousand and one questions about our costumes and *Alice's Adventures in Wonderland*. "Lucy's father left when she was like two, and my Aunt Ana likes for her to have some, you know, male role models around." He shrugs his shoulders like he's embarrassed.

"That's real sweet of you," I say.

Danny tilts his head to the side, and the light rests fully on his face. I notice that he's shaved. His curly hair is barely wavy, flattened by the weight of his mask.

"That wig makes you look different," he says.

Automatically, I tug on the ends to straighten it. I like the way I look in this wig. My hair isn't so crazy, and my face looks less angular.

"No, it doesn't."

"Yeah, it does." He looks at me, and I feel like he can almost see right through me, which is stupid, I know. It's just sometimes I feel like I might be able to be comfortable around him, which is a huge step for me. I can barely be comfortable around myself.

He closes his eyes, rubbing his temples. "Would you mind dimming the lights a little?"

"Do you have a headache?"

"Feels like it," Danny says.

I turn off the lights, and we sit in the dark. He rests his head on the cushion. With his eyes closed, I take in the contours of his face. I imagine what it would be like to run my fingers through his hair, to inhale his scent, to see if he tastes like Zest, to do all those things that I read about in Leslie's *Cosmo* magazines.

"It's nothing." He opens his eyes and catches me staring at him.

"Huh?"

"The headache is nothing, really." He closes his eyes again and massages his temples.

"Is it a tension headache?" I ask. "Because if it is, there's this point between your eyebrows here"—I point to the indentation in the center of my eyebrows between my nose and my forehead—"called the third eye, and if you press it just right, the tension should go away."

"Yeah?" He shakes his head at me. "How do you know?"

"It's called acupressure. It's ancient," I say, my confidence in this subject suddenly shaky. "It's Chinese." I add for clarity, "Like from China."

"That's like Asian. Like in Asia?" He asks with a smile.

I nod my head stupidly, even though I know he's teasing me.

"Can you do it?" His voice is low and slippery.

"Me? No . . ." I shake my head. What have I gotten myself into? "I've never actually done it. I've just seen it done . . . to my dad—"

"By a real doctor?"

In the family room, Marisol and Lucy are laughing over a Charlie Brown cartoon special, and I wonder why I'm not with them. Why am I here? ALONE? With Danny?

"No, my mom. She studied holistic medicine in nursing school. She used to do it to my dad."

"Used to?" He rolls his head along the side of the cushion and opens his eyes. The noise from the television fills the space between us, and I look away slowly.

"Do you think you could do it to me?" he asks.

"Now?" I whisper.

"Yeah," he says, his voice catching in his throat. "Now."

"I don't know," I retreat farther into the cushions of my seat. "It works on my dad, but I'm not sure that it would work on you."

"Why don't we try?" I watch him eliminate the safe space between us. He sits on the floor and, like it's the most natural thing in the world, rests his head on my thigh.

We are touching.

"I . . . don't think I can . . ." The missing pieces of my sentence float out the open window into the cool October air.

"Here." He reaches back for my hands. He places them on his forehead between his eyebrows. "Please . . ." His voice is as thick as honey.

I press my finger on his third eye and hold. My thighs squeeze together. I think, *There is a boy shuddering between my thighs.*

And like that—I stop breathing. My heart stops beating. My body takes one huge pause. And I wonder how things like this, unexpected things, can happen so quickly and make me feel so alive.


that's how marisol finds us. five minutes later, when the doorbell rings, she passes through our moment and finds Danny still sitting at the base of my feet. When she reaches to unlock the front door, we untangle ourselves.

I turn on the lights. Marisol takes charge. She speaks to Lucy's mother, makes the proper introductions, returns Lucy's wet clothes, and ushers Danny out the door. Then she flicks off the light and tells me to follow her. But I can't. If I move, I might lose the feeling of Danny's body so close to mine.

So I sit alone in the dark, and, for the first time in my entire life, I experience what it is to ache.

# ELEVEN

# truth or dare

• • •

around midnight, marisol persuades me to play truth or dare. It's a game that we play on a regular basis. It's our way of catching up with each other. But tonight it feels dangerous. I make sure to go first. The plan is to steer the conversation past Danny Diaz, past his head resting on my thigh.

"Truth or dare," I begin, lighting several candles perched delicately on Marisol's nightstand table.

"Truth."

"Do you think your mom likes my dad?"

"Yes," Marisol replies quickly. "My turn. Why was Dan—"

"Really? You think so?" The answer makes me feel uncomfortable. "Why?" My dad is a hermit crab. Why does she like him?

"It's my turn," Marisol says, ignoring my question.

"But, it's a quick question to answer."

"The rules," Marisol snaps. "Stop breaking the rules."

"Fine," I say with a glare, "but I don't appreciate your tone."

"Whatever. Truth or dare?"

"Dare."

"Huh?" Marisol gives me a suspicious look. "You've never picked dare before."

"Dare," I repeat.

"Okay, I dare you . . ."—she gives me a wicked smile—"to drink water from the toilet bowl."

"What?" Secret or no secret, I wasn't drinking water from a toilet bowl. "That's crazy."

"No." Marisol stands up. "It's a dare. It's supposed to be daring."

"Well, I'm not sticking my face in a toilet bowl."

"Yes, you are."

"No," I tell her, "I'm not! You can't give me something really gross as a dare."

"It's not gross. My dog drinks water from the toilet bowl, and dogs have the cleanest mouths in the world."

"Your dog eats her own shit!"

"And she washes it down with toilet water." She pauses dramatically. "Okay, I dare you . . . to make out with Danny Diaz."

"You can't dare that—"

"Why? Because he's super-ugly, right?"

"I didn't say that!" I protest.

"So . . . then he's cute?"

"The whole school thinks he's cute. It's not my opinion," I exclaim. "It's a fact!"

"Well," Marisol says calmly, "according to the rules you can't back down on a dare that's not gross. So this Wednesday when you tutor him, you have to absolutely make out with him—"

"You can't force me to make out with some guy on a dare." My voice rises. "And you know that we have a professional relationship. A professional relationship!" I scream so loudly that Lola, their dog, starts howling outside.

"A professional relationship? Hah!" Marisol points accusingly in the direction of the living room. "Since when does 'professional tutoring' involve sitting with your *pupil* between your *thighs*?"

"He had a tension headache! I was applying my fingers to his third eye."

"More like his third leg—"

"Wh—what?" My mouth flops to the floor. "That's just gross."

"Well, hey," she says in a whiny voice, "where can I get a dumb, hot soccer player with tension headaches? I want one of those!"

"So you admit he's hot?" I thrust my finger accusingly in her face.

"Hellooooo?" Marisol flicks me in the nose, and the tension cracks.

"You're such an über-bitch," I tell her.

"I know." Marisol plops down on her bed, and we both bust out laughing.

"Were you really going to make me drink toilet water?"

"Yep."

"Make out with Danny Diaz?"

"Yep."

"Why do you think whenever we use his first name in a sentence, we follow it with his last?"

"Because it sounds cool," she says.

"Yep."

"So, scoop." Marisol curls up in a ball and tucks her pillow between her thighs. "What's going on between you and Danny Diaz?"

"Nothing . . ."

"C'mon," she prods.

"Nothing . . . I mean it."

"Then take truth," she says.

"Okay"—my upper lip trembles—"truth."

"Do you," she asks quietly, "like Danny Diaz?"

I hesitate, which is all but verbal confirmation of my feelings. A part of me wants to say yes, but the feelings are so new that I'm not exactly sure how to own up to them.

"I like tutoring him." I give her the safest reply I can muster.

"Hmm . . ." She fixes her eyes on me. "Okay, just answer yes or no to the following questions. Okay?"

I nod yes.

"You liked touching him?" she asks slowly.

Did I like touching Danny Diaz? I think about my hands coursing through Danny's soft hair. I inhale the palm of my hand to see if I can still smell him. I nod yes.

"Did he touch you?"

"Yes." I look up at the ceiling. I remember Danny's hand reaching for mine.

"So, duh"—a grin flashes across her face—"you like him."

I nod my head because it's true. I like Danny Diaz.

"Now," she says with a wicked smile, "the question is, does he make you tingle?"

"Don't be stupid." I throw a stuffed animal at her, which she skill-fully dodges. "People don't tingle."

Marisol gives me a doubtful look.

"Have you ever tingled?" I ask.

"This isn't about me. This is about you."

"Whatever," I say, because of course Danny doesn't make me tingle. But when I'm around him, I do feel something else. I guess I feel okay, like really, really okay, which is saying a lot.

"Why are you so excited about who I like?" I bury my face in the part of her comforter that smells like strawberries.

"I'm not." She purses her lips like she's thinking.

"Are you coming off a sugar high?"

"No . . . I'm just happy for you. Is there something wrong with that?"

"No, except there's nothing to be happy for."

"Not yet"—she gives me a strange smile—"but soon."

In the candlelight, Marisol looks a lot like her mom. They both have eyes like saucers, long narrow noses, and swollen pink lips. But it's the symmetry of their faces that makes it work. It just all adds up. And sometimes, like now, as the light flickers across her face, Marisol can be breathtaking.

Not like me.

"Do you think I look like my mother?" I ask Marisol.

"Huh?" Marisol rolls over on her bed and looks at me. "What brought that on?"

"Oh"—I stare at my reflection in the mirror opposite me—"I don't know. Do you think that I do?"

"Well . . ." Marisol stares at me for a long time. "I don't know." She tilts a candle so that the melting wax drips onto her skin. "It's been a long time, you know."

"Yeah," I say quietly, "I know." I close my eyes and try to conjure up an image of my mother. But I can't.

I can't.

# TWELVE

# secrets

. . .

wednesday, november ninth.

IT HAPPENS. The world, specifically Ryan Rosenbloom, figures out the one thing that I already know. Marisol is beautiful.

"I said yes," Marisol sighs and smiles. She is in heaven. We're eating lunch in Siberia, which, technically, is a canal five minutes away
from school.

Her head rests on her book bag. Her hand stretches to the sky,
tracing a cloud that passes overhead. All around us ducks screech,
diving after crumbs thrown from the old man's bag.

"What do you think his name really is?" Marisol nods toward the
old man.

"I thought we agreed it was Carlos," I tell her impatiently. I want
to get back to our prior conversation. I want to know more.

"God. What is it with you and your stereotypes? His name could
be Bob. How do we even know he's Hispanic?" She raises an eyebrow
inquisitively as if we're discussing philosophy or some other great big
mystery of the universe.

"You've seen the way he dresses. The guayabera, the straw

hats . . . I guess he could be Bahamian or Jamaican." I shake my head. "Stop trying to change the subject."

"The lake is absolutely lovely today." Marisol eyes Siberia. She's practically glowing.

"It's a man-made canal," I tell her. "There's nothing lovely about it."

"Yes, there is." She smiles again, and I want to shove my sub down her throat. What right does she have to be so happy? What right does she have getting asked to homecoming? I didn't know the thing existed until today when Marisol told me that Ryan Rosenbloom asked her.

"You should go," she tells me all casually. "It'll be fun."

I look at her eager expression, and I want to crush her. "Let's see," I say, my tone equally casual, "I'll just select one lucky guy from my many admirers, find the perfect dress, and have an absolutely *lovely* time."

"You don't have to make fun of me." Her voice oozes deflation.

"You're right, I don't, but I am." I choose my next words carefully. "Marisol, what's happening to us? We don't do dances."

"We," she says, her voice slightly clipped, "don't do *anything*. That's the problem."

"That's so not true!" I say, but maybe it is? "Besides, didn't Ryan's best friend call you 'brace face' for all of seventh grade?"

Marisol's eyes narrow. "Ryan hasn't been best friends with Jeff Henderson since eighth grade. So what's your point?"

"Well, Ryan never defended you. That's my point. Seriously"—my voice drips with false concern—"how can you trust a guy like that?"

"Well"—Marisol squishes her eyebrows—"correct me if I'm wrong, but you never defended me either."

"Yeah"—I squish my eyebrows back at her—"but that's because Jeff used to call me 'caterpillar face.' And"—I rub the now hair-free space between my eyebrows—"that was a very traumatic experience for me."

"Whatever." Marisol smiles victoriously. "That makes Ryan and you one and the same."

"Whatever." I pout in silence.

"What's your problem?"

"Nothing," I tell her, which is a lie.

I watch Carlos. Or Bob. Or whatever his name is. I wonder if he ever went to homecoming. Or maybe he's one of the last people in America who understands what it's like to never have a date? But that doesn't make sense, I remind myself, because he has a daughter. We've seen her out here with him. So he's had at least one successful date.

So now I know that there is absolutely no one left in America besides me who understands what it's like to be without a date, or worse, to be without the hope of dating.

I give Marisol a sidelong glare. Marisol used to understand everything, but now she wants my father to date her mother, and she wants to go to freaking dances and sit with the Jewish clique and forget me.

"You're sure?" she asks.

"Sure about what?" I toss out the attitude.

"Not going. I think Ryan's cousin Jared doesn't have a date." Marisol's voice trails up hopefully. "Or at least he mentioned that to me before."

"That must have been one long conversation." Today is the first day Marisol ever mentioned talking to Ryan, but now she was using words like *before*?

"Why?" she looks confused.

"For him to feel comfortable enough to mention his lonely, half-retarded cousin." I watch her shift uncomfortably on the grass. "I'm just saying he must have felt extremely comfortable with you."

"Well . . ." She picks nervously at a weed.

"Well, what?"

"Ryan's been calling me since the middle of October." She doesn't lift her eyes from the weed.

"That's like a month ago," I say slowly.

"I know."

"So you've been keeping this from me. Why?"

I search her face for clues. When did we become the type of best friends to keep things from each other? What happened to our truth nights, to knowing everything? Why the secrets?

"I don't know." She shrugs her shoulders. "I don't want to keep stuff from you. Just, lately, I want to *do* stuff. I want to go out. And you always want to stay in." She lifts her eyes back to mine.

I don't know what to say. I mean, what can I say? It's kinda true. But it's not my fault that I don't want to go out. I just don't like crowds. I don't like people. People are . . . well, they can be scary sometimes.

"But why couldn't you tell me that before?" My voice cracks, just a little.

"I don't know." Marisol taps a finger under my chin so that I'll look at her. "I wanted to wait until . . ."

"Until what?" I prompt her.

"I thought for sure that Danny would ask you to homecoming. I thought that if Danny asked you, well then you might really go. And we could do something fun for once."

"Oh." I'm spinning. My mind is processing like a hundred thoughts but one sticks out: she thinks we never do anything fun together. She's bored of me.

"We could still go to the dance together," she says.

"Oh." There's not much else to say.

"I just wanted us to belong for once." Her voice wavers.

"Oh."

"Is that all you can say?" She snaps.

"No," I say rather quietly.

The truth is there is a lot more that I could say, like *What's wrong with you? When did you stop liking me, start lying to me? Where are you going? Where am I going? Are we going to stop being . . .*

No, I can't say that. I can't even *think* that.

I study her carefully. I try to think of one moment in my life that she has ever let me down (not hurt my feelings, but actually let me down), and I can't. So I suck it up. Marisol has the right to be happy, even if it gives me heartburn.

"I think it's great," I say finally.

"Really?" She gives my hand a gentle squeeze. I bite my lip to stop myself from saying, *Don't go. Don't leave me alone.*

"Yeah, I really do."

"Good." Marisol smiles, and her blue eyes twinkle in the sun. "I'm super-excited," she says.

"Yeah, it's great." I nod my head and force a smile.

But I don't think it's great. In fact, I think the whole thing sucks.

# THIRTEEN

# what about me?

•  •  •

later that afternoon before i meet danny for our afternoon tutorial, I hide out in the girls' restroom and stare at myself in the mirror. What does Marisol have that I don't have? Why does Marisol get to have a boyfriend and I don't? And when did I start caring about these sorts of things?

I try to remind myself that Ryan isn't Marisol's boyfriend, that all they're doing is hanging out. Secretly hanging out. My mind gets stuck on the word *secretly*. And it's somewhere along that point that I convince myself that Marisol has a boyfriend, and life as I know it is about to end.

I hate my life. I do.

*Do I hate my life?*

Well, not all the time, but there are certain moments, seconds of the day that I'm particularly pissed off at God for making my life the way that it is.

The restroom is quiet. I'm thankful for the silence. It's not often during the day that you can actually hear yourself think. And I use this time to undertake one of the most pressing questions in my current life: *what is there for anyone, maybe even Danny, to love about me?*

I stare in the mirror and try to see myself through Danny's eyes. The first thing I do is look into my eyes. Yes, my eyes look like they belong on an owl, but the color is pretty enough, they're brown with flecks of green.

What about my nose? It's long and narrow. My dad says that it is Romanesque. Anything that's Romanesque can't be good.

My lips are full, maybe too full, like fish lips.

Ugly.

I take my time walking downstairs while I continue to catalog my body.

In the stairwell, I think about my hips. They're too wide. I'll probably give birth to twins—that is, of course, if I ever have sex.

I also observe my breasts. Very small, but I think that's preferable to the watermelons that Pamela Anderson is toting around. Breasts definitely shouldn't be bigger than your head.

The first floor is empty. I don't even hear the echo of a conversation. I stop in front of a full-length window display and stare at my reflection in the Plexiglas.

I check out my legs. I'm all about the leg. They're super-long, which may not be an attribute now, as growing boys can be intimidated by female giants, but in the future they'll definitely come in handy. One point for me.

I turn sideways, lift up my shirt and admire my stomach. It's so flat, it's concave. Boys like a girl with a flat stomach. I'm up to two.

When it comes to my upper arms, I don't bother to flex. My biceps have always been nonexistent. Although I don't think I can be penalized for that; biceps just don't run in my family. My grandmother's biceps have always hung upside down. But they are skinny, which is better than flabby, right? Okay, I'll take half a point.

My eyes travel down and around the back. My crown, my glory—my butt. In the Plexiglas, my butt looks very nice. It's perky, heart shaped, and full. I fill out the back pockets of my jeans completely. A perfect butt should be worth three points alone. I mean look how far J. Lo's butt has gotten her. I should be so lucky to attract half as many husbands based on my perky cheeks.

Okay. I do the math in my head.

| | |
|---|---|
| Super-long legs: | 1 point |
| Concave stomach: | 1 point |
| Skinny, bicepless arms: | 0.5 point |
| J. Lo butt: | 3 points |

Five and a half points. That's my total. Which means what? On a scale of one to ten, I'm five and a half. Five and a half? That's bad. That's real bad. Wait. No, that can't be right. I didn't list ten body parts. The equation has to be equal to the number of body parts being examined or it won't be mathematically sound, but then again—

A shadow falls across the Plexiglas and startles me. After an involuntary squeal, which I have the feeling that I'll regret for the rest of my life, I find myself face to glass-face with Danny.

"How . . ." I fight to gain my composure. "How . . . long have you been standing there?"

Did he see me staring at myself? Evaluating myself?

He lets out a low laugh. "I've been here like a minute." He taps his fingers on the Plexiglas. "What are you looking at?" He stares at the display. "Are you going to homecoming?"

"What?" I try to keep my voice steady. "Why?"

"Um . . . I don't know. You're standing in front of a homecoming display."

He points toward the window case, and for the first time, I notice what it says inside: FALL INTO FUN ON SATURDAY, NOVEMBER 19. Underneath the caption is a picture of a couple in formal wear posing happily for the camera. Just seeing the camera makes me shudder.

"Oh. . . ." I recover my composure. "Yeah, right."

"So you are?"

"What?"

"Going . . ."

"Where?"

"To homecoming."

"Homecoming?" I reply evasively.

"Susie . . ." Danny's smile fades, but his tone is still lighthearted.

I wish he would just drop the whole conversation. I feel like I can barely breathe. What does he care? Unless . . . but the chances of Danny asking me to homecoming are zilch. He could ask anyone. Why would he want to ask me?

"No," I tell him. "I'm not . . . going."

"You're not going?" he repeats.

"No."

"You're not going to homecoming?"

"No," I say for the second time, "I'm not." Why does he insist on making me repeat myself?

"This homecoming." He taps the Plexiglas.

"Yes," I say very slowly. "I am not going to that homecoming."

"Oh," he says with a smile.

"Oh?" Is he happy that I won't be there?

"Your eye is twitching." He leans forward and touches the corner of my eye, where a pulsation has just erupted.

"Can we go?" I ask impatiently.

"Yeah." He smiles again, annoying me even further.

"Good." I walk in front of him toward the library.

"Wait." He lays his hand on my shoulder and I jump. "The library is closed."

"What?" I drop my bag on the ground. "You're joking. Why?"

He shrugs his shoulders. "The sign said inventory. But don't worry, we'll go somewhere else."

"We don't have anywhere else to go." My eye twitch increases.

"Well, what about Mr. Murphy's classroom?" he suggests.

I glance at my watch. It's already after three thirty.

"No, Mr. Murphy leaves at three, unless you make an appointment with him. Maybe we should just do this tomorrow?" I'd much rather be at home right now analyzing every single word that we've exchanged than discussing *The Scarlet Letter*. I mean, really, why would he bring up homecoming?

"Or we could go to your house?" Danny counters.

It takes a second for the question to register. He wants to come to my house? That would be his second visit in, like, thirty days.

The truth is that ever since Halloween, all I can think about is Danny coming over to my house. Danny in my room. But having a fantasy and seeing it through are two different things.

"I don't think that's such a good idea," I say after much internal debate. "My dad's working at home."

We lean against a row of lockers. Danny runs his fingers through his hair, and his movement triggers more memories of Halloween. I'm flooded. And I think about touching him.

"Well, how about my house? I live only two blocks away."

"Oh, I don't know." There are so many questions running through my head right now. What if he invites me into his room? What would it be like to see his bed or smell his sheets? What would it be like to know what his comforter looks like or see his closet filled with clothes? That information alone might keep me up late at night. I just don't think I can handle the pressure of being at his house.

I rack my brain for a foolproof excuse. "I'm not really allowed to go to a boy's house if my dad doesn't know him." I force my voice to sound apologetic. How weird would I feel meeting Dalia or his parents?

"Well, your dad and I met the other day, remember?"

"Yeah," I say sarcastically, "but that doesn't constitute knowing." Heck, I've been meeting Danny for more than a month now, and I can't even tell what he means by a simple question.

"If my dad met your parents, that would probably be a different story, but he hasn't."

"Oh." He leans back against the locker and taps his fingers on his head. I wonder if his fingers give him extra brain power. "Okay, I know. My mom gets home from work at four, so I'll have her call your mom to explain."

"You can't call my mom," I began, trying to force the next words out.

"Why not?" Danny asks.

"Because . . ." My mind starts racing. *Just tell him the truth*, I think. But I can't. Not yet. "You just can't," I repeat.

"Okay." Danny seems to consider whether he should push that subject, but he doesn't. "Can we call your dad? You said he's at home. Right?"

"Yeah, you can call my dad." We were treading on dangerous ground, and it seemed better to give in than raise more questions.

"We're just going to be studying, not playing doctor," he says. And my heart goes a thousand times faster.

"I kn-kn-ow." I pause to get the stuttering under control. "I wa-as just thinking that I have to be home by six."

"No prob-buh-blem." He grabs my book bag off the floor. "Let's go."

# FOURTEEN

# la casa diaz

•  •  •

we walk the first block in silence. i sneak sideways glances at him just to watch him carry my bag. I like the way he retrieved it from the floor, without saying a word. The action was very take charge. I dig that.

"It's this way." I follow the right he makes on SW 132nd Avenue, and try to keep up with his long strides. The boy's leg span covers twice the amount of territory of mine. We make a left on SW 65th Street, and my stomach flips. The path we're taking is suddenly becoming very familiar to me.

"Have you ever been here?" Danny asks. He points to a man-made canal. My man-made canal! My designated lunch spot!

"Well?" he prompts.

I look around. My Carlos or Bob (or whatever his name is) is sitting on a bench, reading. Ducks huddle nearby, waiting.

"Kind of." I debate whether to admit that this is my lunch spot. "Marisol and I kind of like to eat here," I mutter underneath my breath. I look over at Carlos. He's starting to feed the ducks. "I think"—I say, pointing at the old man—"all he does is feed ducks all day."

"Huh?" Danny gives me an odd look. He sticks two fingers in his mouth and whistles. The old man smiles and looks up. "*Hola*." Danny waves. "*Qué pasó?*"

"*Nada*." The old man says, crinkly eyed, before disappearing behind the wrinkled folds of an *El Nuevo Herald*.

"What did you say?" I ask. Why didn't I ever think about saying hello?

"I asked him what he's up to. And he said, '*Nada*,' which means 'nothing.'"

"I know what *nada* means. I'm a third-year Spanish student. I mean, why did you say anything to him at all?" We approach a mesh fence that leads into a well-kept backyard that seems familiar. I look back toward the old man, only feet away. "Is he your grandfather?" I ask incredulously, because if that's not a sign from God then I don't know what is.

Danny smiles mysteriously. "You'll see."

We cut through the backyard and enter the house through an unlocked sliding glass door. "Mami?" Danny calls out, but no one answers. "This is the family-room-slash-kitchen. Notice the tile is authentic Italian," Danny says in a nasal voice. "It's a postmodern impressionistic Italian Renaissance style." He gives me a cockeyed grin. "Don't you think I'd be a great real estate agent?"

"No." I roll my eyes. "But I do think you'd make a great farmer because you're so darn corny," I say, which actually makes Danny laugh.

I check out the room. It's not as large as my family room, but it's pretty. The walls are painted mango; the floor tile is a light brown. The largest wall is covered with family portraits. In the center is a large oil painting—of Danny and Dalia kneeling at an altar. Dalia is wearing a plain white dress. Danny is wearing a suit. They both look about twelve in the photo.

"Is that your confirmation picture?" I ask.

"Yeah," he smiles. "Are you Catholic, too?"

"Yeah, but I never actually got to the confirmation part," I tell him.

I turn back to the wall and study some of the other photos. The wall is practically a visual history of Danny's entire life: Danny sitting in a tub filled with bubbles; Danny and Dalia at their kindergarten graduation; his parents' wedding photo; his mom laughing into a camera, holding a big belly.

"Is that your mom when she was pregnant with you two?"

Danny steps closer to look. "Yeah, she was huge."

"What's it like to be a twin?" I am curious.

"It's cool," he says. "People think it makes you different, but it's just like having any other sibling. I guess it's nice to be in the same classes and copy each other's homework—not that Dalia would ever let me copy anything of hers—but sometimes having a sister can be annoying. Are you an only child?"

"Yeah."

"Do you wish you had a brother or a sister?"

I consider the question. For a long time after my mother died, I wondered what it would have been like to have an older sister. I thought maybe she would understand how I was feeling, or maybe she could explain to me why things like this happened—why they happened to us. Even if we didn't talk about other things, maybe we could just play together. Maybe then, I wouldn't be so lonely.

"I used to," I tell him, "but not anymore."

I look from the photos to Danny, then outside to his grandfather reading the paper. I think about his tiny house overlooking the man-made canal with the quacking ducks that crap everywhere. I'm filled with envy.

Danny grabs an apple from a nearby fruit bowl and takes a large bite. "You want a bite?" The apple is so close I can smell it. I nearly die from the thought of our lips touching the same spot.

"It's good," he says, pushing it closer.

"You know," I push the apple away, "that's how Adam got Eve into trouble in the first place."

"I thought it was the other way around."

"Only, if you believe the lies of a patriarchal society," I reply smoothly.

"See," he smiles, "that's what I like about you. You're quick on your feet."

He winks, and I feel myself glowing.

"So, do you want to see my bedroom?" Danny moves toward the hallway.

I shouldn't be surprised—I've read enough *Seventeen* (exactly two issues) to know that it doesn't matter what a girl looks like, a guy always wants to show her his bedroom—but I am.

"Why?"

"Because . . ." Again, Danny gives me a strange look. "That's where my desk is."

"Oh." My cheeks turn red. Silly, silly me.

"Coming?" Danny calls from the hallway.

I take a deep breath and follow.


an hour later, danny's mom comes home. we hear her singing in the kitchen long before she shows her face at Danny's bedroom door. For the past sixty minutes, we've been engrossed in the ending of *The Scarlet Letter*. I've stationed myself and the novel on the floor, while Danny lies on the bed flipping through the CliffsNotes.

"I hate reading," he tells me for the umpteenth time.

"Really? I can't tell." I fold the page and set the book aside. "I think I can read just about anything, except horror. I can't stand those books." I stand and stretch. An hour of reading out loud coupled with in-depth analysis is enough to make my body ache. I bend over and touch my toes. When I straighten up, I notice Danny is watching me.

"So do you think you're ready for your test?" I ask awkwardly.

"Huh?" He shakes his head. I can tell I've caught him off guard.

"Are you ready for your test? Or do you think we need to keep studying?"

"Oh, I'm sorry. Yeah, I think so. You know," he says, suddenly, "you're really bendy." His face is flushed.

"I used to take gymnastics when I was little." I sit at the edge of his bed and draw one knee to my chest. My butt hurts from the hard floor.

"Why'd you stop?" he asks.

"I don't know. I just did." Which is a lie. The truth is I stopped because after my mom died, my dad kept forgetting to take me.

"So you feel prepared?" I ask again.

"How could I not be?" He shakes his head. "You're intense when you study."

"Well"—I make a grave face—"I haven't earned my reputation as a geek for nothing."

"Yeah," he agrees, laughing. "I knew geeks were good for something."

"Yeah," I say, but I can't help but feel a burn. Did he just insult me, or is that supposed to be a compliment? Should I even care? I mean, look where I am. I'm at his house.

But still . . .

"Do you think I'm a geek?" I venture.

The look he gives me, plus his awkward silence, says it all.

"I don't mind," I begin.

"Come on, Susie—"

"No, it's okay."

I stare at the walls of his room, anything to avoid him and his . . . lack of protest.

His room is typical. It's a little messy; there's a swimsuit edition calendar hanging on the wall. A shelf is filled with collectible *Star Wars* action figures, and there are classic film posters everywhere—*Scarface, Lord of the Rings, Star Wars, E.T., The Breakfast Club.*

"Why do you have so many posters?" I pretend to study the *E.T.* poster. I remember the first time my dad rented that movie from Blockbuster. I cried for days.

"I want to be a director," he says rather earnestly.

I look back to him, sitting on the bed, picking the lint from his comforter. I never thought about Danny beyond the context of his being cute and popular. I never thought about his dreams and aspirations. I just thought about how I was beginning to feel about him. Knowing this made me see him a little differently. To be a director, you had to be creative. I never even thought that side of him existed.

"Marisol wants to be a movie critic," I tell him.

"You know what I like about movies?" he says. "I like that we get to see into these characters who are awkward and shy and sometimes they're everything that we feel like on the inside. But instead of hating them like we do in real life, we love them . . . We want them to be happy. Have you ever seen a John Hughes film? He directed *The Breakfast Club* and *Sixteen Candles.*"

"Puh-leeze," I tell him. "Blockbuster practically has me on their VIP list. I've pretty much seen everything John Hughes ever did. And I'm a really big Molly Ringwald fan," I confess.

"Me, too." He shakes his head, and curls fall every which way. I can't take my eyes off him.

"What do you want to be when you grow up?" he asks.

"I don't know." I lean my head against the wall and act like I'm considering the question. The truth is I do know. I've always known. I want to be a songwriter. But I've never shared that information with anyone besides Marisol. "I think I . . ." I almost change my mind, but, once again, I decide to take a chance. "I think I want to be a writer."

"Oh," Danny says. "That's cool. Like your dad, right?" he asks.

"No, not exactly . . . Hey, how did you know my dad's a writer?"

"The same way you seem to know so much about my grandfather." He arches his eyebrows, rolls off the bed, and stands in the doorway. "We'd better call your dad before he starts worrying."

I had forgotten that lie and the time. I smile at the idea that my father might be remotely aware of my absence.

"Let me just go tell my mom, okay? I'll be right back."

When he's gone, I walk over to his bed and lift his pillow to my nose. I inhale deeply and then place it back in exactly the position that I found it. He smells just like I remembered. Like Zest and Neutrogena. I walk back over to the wall with posters and lean against it. I reach into my shirt and pull out the heart-shaped rose quartz that Marisol bought me for my last birthday. It's supposed to bring me good luck. I place it between the palms of my hands and make a wish.

I wish that Danny will be able to one day see inside me and know how I feel. Then I slide down the wall and wait for his return.

# FIFTEEN

# a part of the family

. . .

"susie, this is my mom. mami, this is susie shannon."

Mrs. Diaz is a petite woman with long brown hair and big brown eyes. I've seen her a few times before with Danny's grandfather, but at the time I had no idea who she was, and I've never seen her up close. Now I see that she's about the same height and weight as a junior high student. She's maybe five feet and looks like she barely weighs a hundred pounds. I try to imagine how she carried twins to term and can barely get past the idea that she was ever pregnant.

"Susie?"

When she says my name, I stand. I tower above her, making her seem even more dwarflike. "Mrs. Diaz." I extend my hand to meet hers, but she pulls me forward and gives me a kiss on the cheek.

"I'm happy to finally meet you," she says. "Danny has told us so much about you." My heart skips two beats at the idea of Danny discussing me with his mother before I realize that she's being polite, and I tuck my fantasies away.

"These heels are killing my feet." Mrs. Diaz steps out of her shoes and shrinks two inches. Forget dwarf. This lady is a hobbit.

"Where do you work?" I ask, trying to avoid calling my father for as long as possible.

"I work for the Department of Children and Families."

"Oh . . ." I decide to stall for more time, so I force myself to ask one more question. "Do you like it?"

"Well, let's see . . ." Mrs. Diaz sighs wearily. "I go to work every day and meet lots of abused children and disillusioned families. Oh, and on days like today I get to stay more than an hour late. It's loads of fun."

"Oh," I say, and then I stare at my fingernails. It's one of those awkward moments that I hate.

"But"—Mrs. Diaz places her hand on my forearm, and I wonder if she senses my self-loathing—"I wouldn't give it up for the world. Thanks for asking. So we should call your dad. It's nice to see a parent so concerned."

Danny hands me his cordless phone. I dial my number, hand it over to Mrs. Diaz, and say a little prayer that she won't mention my father's "rules."

"Hi, Mr. Shannon? This is Mrs. Diaz, Danny Diaz's mother. Danny Diaz, uh-huh, that's right, Susie is tutoring my son. . . . I'm fine, and how are you? Great."

I listen closely to the conversation, but try to appear unconcerned by looking around the room casually. Next to me, Danny starts to hum something, but I can barely hear him over the *thump, thump, thump* of my heart.

"Oh, he's doing wonderful. Mr. Murphy thinks he won't need to be tutored after Christmas. Yes, well, the reason for my call is that the school library was closed today and that's where Susie and Danny normally meet. Danny suggested that they come to our house to study. I just wanted to make sure that was okay with you. Yes, uh, okay. Yes, well, thank you. Would you like to talk to her? Yes, she's right here.

One moment . . . Susie?" Mrs. Diaz hands me the phone. "He'd like to speak to you."

after several white lies to my father, i join danny and his mom in the family room. I find them chatting and laughing, and the strange thing is that she's completely into what he's saying.

They make a cute pair. At first, she seems too plain-looking to be his mom, but there are lots of similarities, too. They share the same oval face, defined cheekbones, and angular chins. And there's something else, too. There's something about the way she looks at me, like I could confide in her. It's the same look that Danny gives me, too.

Above them, a picture of Danny's father hangs on the wall. He's handsome like Danny, with the same curly hair and penny-colored eyes. I wonder how this handsome man got together with such a plain, little woman. But maybe it's like Danny said—maybe we're all the same person on the inside? Maybe that's what his dad saw in his mom? Maybe he saw her from the inside out?

I clear my throat to let them know I'm standing there. Their smiles invite me to join in, but I listen quietly. They continue to talk in front of me, and it makes me feel like I'm part of a family. I rarely feel that way, except when I'm with Marisol and her mom.

"Thanks for calling my dad, Mrs. Diaz," I say after a few minutes.

"Oh, you're welcome. Danny says that you're pretty much done studying for the day, so we were thinking that maybe you could stay for dinner."

My heart leaps at the invitation, but my gut tells me to take it slow. Just the thought of asking Dalia to pass the salt makes me queasy, and I start to doubt if Danny even wants me to stay. What if his mother is just being polite? I look at his face. His expression is vague.

"Oh, I'd like to, but," I repeat my earlier excuse, "I've got this thing—this project, and I have to be home by six."

"Oh, yeah," Danny says. "I completely forgot."

"Oh." Mrs. Diaz sounds disappointed. "Well, maybe another time? I know Danny's father would love to meet you."

Danny's father would love to meet me? My stomach flip-flops.

"I know!" Mrs. Diaz says with a smile. "We have plans for this weekend, but why don't you have dinner with us next Sunday?"

"Um . . ." Again, my heart jumps at the invitation. Again, I'm filled with doubt. "I don't know—"

"Oh," Danny laughs, "here she goes again."

"What's that supposed to mean?" Mrs. Diaz asks.

"Mom, Susie doesn't like going places. I practically had to drag her here to study."

I smile shyly because it's true.

"Okay," I say reluctantly. "Next Sunday will be fine."

"Good. We'll have dinner at seven p.m.," Mrs. Diaz says decisively. "You can come over at six fifteen. That'll give you and Danny some time to hang out." Mrs. Diaz nods her head. "What do you like to eat?"

"Cuban food?" I take a shot in the dark.

"Good answer"—Mrs. Diaz laughs—"because my father won't have it any other way. So, we'll see you next Sunday at six fifteen p.m."

"Six fifteen," I repeat shakily.

"Wonderful." Mrs. Diaz claps her hands together in excitement. "I'll look forward to hearing your version of homecoming. Dalia and Danny always have opposite views on school events. It'll be nice to hear from a third party." Mrs. Diaz squeezes Danny's hand lovingly.

"Actually," I glance down at my feet. "I'm not going."

"Oh, I thought that—" She stops short and exchanges a look with Danny. "I mean"—she clears her throat—"I assumed that you would be going, too. Dalia made it seem like one of the biggest events of the year."

"So, you're going to the dance?" I ask Danny

"Um, yeah . . ." He seems embarrassed to admit it. "Dalia persuaded me. She's a homecoming princess and all."

"Oh," I say. I can hear the letdown in my voice, and I hate myself for it. Why am I so stupid? Why do I feel like somebody just slapped me with a huge disappointment stick?

"Of course, Dalia and Danny bought their tickets ages ago," Mrs. Diaz explains. "Dalia was worried the dance would sell out. She's got the whole thing planned, down to a by-the-minute itinerary."

"Yeah," Danny says. "It's ridiculous."

They keep talking, but it's not like I really hear them. I'm still being hit over and over again with the big, fat disappointment stick. I'm surprised I'm still standing, the beating I'm taking.

"Is something wrong?" Mrs. Diaz places her hand on my arm. "Your eyes are all red."

Great.

"Oh, no." It's a struggle, but I make my voice sound calm. "I'm . . . fine." If *fine* means that I want to hurl. Why did I let myself feel so accepted in Danny's home, when the truth is that I'll never fit into his life?

"I don't know." Mrs. Diaz places a hand on my forehead. "You look flushed. Why don't you sit down, and I'll bring you some aspirin and water."

I start to protest, but Mrs. Diaz shoves me on the sofa before I can finish my sentence. Then she rushes off, somewhere in the vicinity of her bedroom, leaving Danny and me sort of, kind of, alone.

"Are you sure you're okay?" Danny sits next to me on the sofa. He tries to put his hand on my forehead, but I dodge it, leaving his hand hanging awkwardly in the air before he slowly sets it down on the sofa.

"Yeah." My voice is terse. "I'm fine."

*Why am I so transparent?*

Danny gives me a look, like he doesn't believe me. But I guess he decides to change the subject, because then he says, "I like your pendant."

I look down. My pendant is resting on the outside of my shirt.

"It's cool." He lifts it up. "That's a crystal, right? What's it for?"

His hand brushes against my collarbone, and my heart does this crazy pitter-patter thing. "What do you mean?" I look away, angry at myself for not being able to control my reaction to him.

"Well . . ." Danny stops, and then starts again. "I just mean, aren't crystals supposed to, like, stand for something?"

I shrug my shoulders and stare off into the kitchen. "Marisol gave it to me . . . so . . ." I mutter, rather lamely.

He rubs it between his fingertips. "It's nice."

"Yeah, thanks." I breathe deeply. Even though I refuse to look at him, I can feel the heat escaping through the pores of his fingertips.

"Susie?" He starts tugging on the chain, and doesn't stop until I finally look back at him. He lets the necklace drop back onto my chest. "Are you sure you're okay?"

His face is sincere, and it melts my iciness a little.

"Yeah," I say a bit more subdued. "I'm fine. Really."

"Good." He gives me a sweet smile. "'Cause I want to ask you something."

Ask me something? Ask ME something?

And that's when I start praying with my eyes open. It's ridiculous and utterly girly, but I can't help it. I start praying: *Please ask me to homecoming. Please ask me to homecoming. Please ask me to homecoming.*

"Yeah?" It's about all I can get out right now.

"Well," he starts out, and suddenly he seems less confident than I've ever seen him before. He's looking down at his knee and picking at his jeans. In the kitchen, I hear his mother start making all kinds of noise, and I wonder, how long does it take to find aspirin and get a freaking glass of water? And why won't she go away already?

"I just," he continues, still picking away at his denim jeans, "I just . . . Um . . ."

Why is he so nervous? My stomach tightens. *Could it be?*

"Yeah," I prod, unusually bold.

"Um." He looks up, and I nod. Finally, he says, "I just want to know what you think about homecoming."

"Well—" And despite the fact that I want more than anything for him to ask me to homecoming, I can't stop the knee-jerk response that railroads out of my mouth. "It's kind of lame and elitist, don't you think?"

Crap! Why did I say that? I mean, I think it's true, but why did I actually say it aloud? Am I so used to being excluded from these types of events that my self-protective responses have become automatic?

"Oh." He starts to pick at the lint on the sofa. "Oh," he says again. And then he just shakes his head, like now it all makes sense to him. Only I don't want what I've said to make sense to him. I want him to ask me the question all over again, because clearly I answered it COMPLETELY wrong.

"Oh," he says, "so you don't want to go? Do you?"

I vigorously shake my head no—because that's not true, I do want to go. I mean, I'd want to go, if someone like Danny asked me.

I mean, sure, before today, I didn't even really know about homecoming. I didn't even really know about guys asking girls out. I mean, I knew that guys asked girls out. Of course, I knew that. But I never knew that guys asked girls like me and Marisol out. But now that I know that girls like Marisol (and, therefore, girls like me) could get asked out to things like homecoming, I definitely want to go. I don't have the power to articulate it, but I definitely want to go.

"Susie?"

"Yes, Danny?" Okay, this is the moment. This is the moment. I try to focus, so I can get it right this time.

"You can stop shaking your head no. I get it."

"Huh?"

At first, I don't understand what he's saying.

"You," he says, and he physically grabs my head to hold it in place, "can stop shaking your head no. I get that you think homecoming is a stupid, elitist event. Okay?"

And then I realize the whole time that I've been shaking my head no, but meaning yes, Danny thought that I meant no. I just said no twice to the same question! I'm retarded. Clearly, I'm retarded.

In the kitchen, Mrs. Diaz finally turns on the faucet, and just the sound of water running makes me cough, my throat is so dry. A little farther off, a door opens and slams shut, and I can't help it; my head automatically shoots up at the sound, and I hear Danny say, "Dalia's home." Then he shifts a few spaces away from me and stops talking and picking altogether. And I realize that it's over. The moment is gone. I blew it.

I look over my shoulder. I can barely speak; my throat's like sandpaper. "Will she come in here?" I ask, and then I move more than a few spaces away, I move a mile away from him, because if he's going to reject me, then I'm going to reject him, too.

"Probably." Danny shakes his head and squints his eyes at me, but his voice stays pretty neutral. "But first, she'll change and call her boyfriend. You've never met Dalia, right?" he asks, rubbing his temple.

I shake my head no, and this time I actually mean no. I'm also pretty sure that now is not the time for intros. I just want to go home. I just want to go home and wallow. Danny's not going to ask me to homecoming, that's obvious. "Can you—can you get my stuff?"

"Yeah." Danny looks slightly put out, and I wonder if maybe I misjudged him AGAIN. But then he says, rather roughly, "Yeah, I guess we're . . . done." And then I know that I didn't.

When Danny leaves, Mrs. Diaz FINALLY brings me a huge glass of water that I suck down in one sip. I try to calm myself by watching her bustle around the kitchen. It doesn't work.

"Here you go." Danny comes back a few minutes later and hands me my things. "Oh, and"—he produces two CDs from behind his back—"I burned these for you."

"Huh?" I shake my head.

"It's the Beatles," he says, like I'm slow, and he's grumpy.

He burned ME a CD? If I believed for a second that signs existed, I might say this was a sign—THE SIGN. But that seemed impossible.

"Remember two weeks ago you told me you liked them?"

I think back to two weeks ago, but I only vaguely recall a conversation where maybe—in passing—I mentioned that Marisol and I kind of liked old-school stuff like the Beatles.

"I made one for you and one for Marisol." He shrugs. "My parents have a huge Beatles collection, so . . ." He stops. Then he mutters the rest, like it's all one big word: "Ijustwantedtothankyouforhelpingme-onthattestandforotherthings." He shoves his hands into his pockets.

"Yeah, well it's . . ." I take a deep breath and go for it. "Sweet." And when he looks up at me and smiles, sort of, I think, *maybe I can do this?* Maybe *I can* turn this around?

I'm about to set my book bag back on the floor when he says, "I guess I'll see you next week?" And then he turns and opens the sliding glass door.

"Oh," I hesitate, because now I'm unsure. I walk toward the sliding glass door, not really ready to leave, but not really sure what to say so that I can stay. I'd like to tell him how much his CD means to me; how special he has made me feel; and that I'm absolutely sure that if he were to ask me to homecoming, I'd say yes. And that's when I find myself saying his name.

"Danny?"

"Yeah?" He smiles, and his eyes seem so gentle and open again.

"I . . ." I struggle to speak. I struggle to get past the doubting voice in the back of my head that says, how can Danny ever like someone like me? How can Danny like someone who's not anything?

"Yeah?" Danny says again.

"I just wanted to say—"

In the background, I hear Dalia talking to Mrs. Diaz. Their voices are coming closer and closer. My heart beats faster and faster. Danny hears them, too. He looks over his shoulder and takes the slightest step away from me.

"Yeah?" he asks for the third time, and maybe it's me, but I think he sounds a little impatient.

I try to read him, but I can't. I can't, and that's when I stop trying because the answer is so obviously clear. I say, "Oh, nothing. Just thanks. Thanks for everything."

And then I leave, wishing that—despite the most embarrassing consequences—I might have had the courage to say more.

# SIXTEEN

# catfight

· · ·

the next day in driver's ed, i sit in my squad line and think about everything Marisol had to say the day before. I think about wanting to fit in. What makes that so important to Marisol or even to me?

I've always considered myself logical enough to know that after high school none of these people will matter. But because I've spent pretty much the last eleven years with them, I can't help but wonder if maybe that's a lie. What if they always matter? What if later on in life—just like now—I don't fit in? Does Marisol feel that way, too?

"Let's go!" Jessica nudges me with her shoe. José is absent, so for today, she's squad leader. We're parallel parking, which according to Coach Brown, is the eighth wonder of the world.

I shake my head. "I don't feel well."

"Well . . ." she says snottily, "I didn't ask for the explanation. Come on, Bobby, you're on!"

"God," Tamara says after Jessica's dragged Bobby away. "I can't believe that she and I have to be on the same homecoming court. She's such a super-bitch. I can't believe that Danny ever dated someone like her."

"What?" I turn around so quickly, I nearly get whiplash. "What did you say?"

"Yeah," Tamara's eyes widen gleefully. "You didn't know? As soon as Danny got here last year, she snatched him up. They broke up in August, I think."

"How do you know?" I strain to sound disinterested.

"Everyone knows, and Danny"—she drops her eyes slyly—"told me last night when he came over to my house."

"Danny . . . came . . . to . . . your house . . . last night?" I repeat slowly.

"Yeah." Her smile is so bright, I'm almost blinded. "We've been studying for our SATs together since right before Halloween. You know"—she leans in so that I can smell every crevice of her peppermint breath—"ever since you told him that I wanted to know if he had a girlfriend."

"Oh." I don't know whether to claw her eyes out or pound my head into the cement for being such an idiot.

What did Danny say when he gave me the CD? *Thank you for helping me with my test and for other things . . .* By *other things*, did he mean hooking him up with Tamara?

"Yeah, I really, really wanted to thank you. I can't believe it. He's like super-super-hot! Don't you think? Anyway," Tamara continues, "I've been dying to tell Jessica, but I haven't had a chance. I can't wait to see the look on her face!"

The clouds clear and the sunlight highlights Tamara's honey-colored tones. Next to my pile of frizz, her hair is bone straight. Jennifer Aniston straight.

What was it that Danny said about my *Alice in Wonderland* wig? *You look so different . . .* I guess I did—I looked more like Tamara.

"Oh." Tamara rolls her eyes. "Look who's coming."

I look up to see Jessica approaching. Her jet-black hair blows in the wind as she struts toward us like the whole world is watching her—or at least every guy in our class. If Danny is into bitchy, gorgeous girls with mammoth breasts, I can see why Jessica appeals to him.

"When Jessica gets here," Tamara whispers in my ear, "ask me who invited me to homecoming. It'll be totally funny."

"Who invited you?" My stomach drops a thousand feet. "Who invited you?" I repeat.

Tamara rolls her eyes. Again. "Just ask . . . Here she comes."

"Let's go." Jessica nudges Tamara with her foot. "It's your turn."

"Sorry," Tamara says politely, "but Susie was just in the middle of asking me a question, so you'll have to wait." She turns back to me and says very loudly, "What was your question?"

"What?" I feel numb.

"Your question . . ." Tamara smiles sweetly, but her eyes are slowly narrowing. "Remember?"

Jessica plants her hands on her hips and looks down at us. "Can you hurry this up? You're holding everyone up."

Tamara pinches me. "C'mon," she hisses.

"Looks like you're ready, so let's go." Jessica taps the top of Tamara's head like she's tapping a table.

It seems impossible that Danny would go out with either of these über-bitches. But, apparently he would. He would go out with them, but not with me, never with me.

"Actually," I say suddenly, "I do have a question." I stand up so that I tower over both of them. "Tamara, when did you become such a bitch?"

I glare down at Tamara. Her mouth drops open and she stares at me with a dumbstruck expression. Behind me, Jessica bursts out laughing.

"You think this is funny?" I turn toward Jessica. Then I look back at Tamara, still staring up at me, her jaw glued to the floor. "You two deserve each other."

"What?" Jessica stops laughing. "What did you say?" She takes a step toward my face like she's about to hit me, and I seriously debate backing down. Adrenaline is pumping through my veins. I'm totally shaking from the inside out. But it's like I can't stop myself. It's like having an out-of-body experience or something. All I can think is what evil bitches Tamara and Jessica really are.

"Jessica—" Instinctively, I step back. "Tamara has something she wants you to know."

Jessica turns toward Tamara and hisses, "What?"

Tamara stares up at us, quivering.

"Tamara, tell us who you are going to homecoming with," I command.

Tamara looks from Jessica to me and then back to Jessica, completely aware that she's being sabotaged.

"Who are you going with, Tamara?" Jessica kicks Tamara's thigh.

"Ouch!" Tamara is stunned, utterly stunned.

"Well, who?" Jessica kicks her again. "Who?"

It's like watching a cat about to be eaten by a dog, only worse.

"I'm going with Danny . . ." Tamara stutters. "Danny Diaz."

"Excuse me?" Jessica crouches over Tamara. "Excuse me," she coils her head like a snake. "You're going where with Danny?"

"She"—I enunciate my words carefully so Jessica will get the full impact—"is going to homecoming with Danny Diaz. Your ex-boyfriend." Then I take ten steps back and wait for the sparks to fly.

And they do fly. There's glistening hair going everywhere.

It takes exactly thirty seconds for Jessica's screaming and Tamara's shrieking to draw the attention of the entire class.

"What's going on?" Bobby sidles up to me as the rest of the class starts to crowd around.

"I think," I say with a smile, "I just ignited the first catfight of the year."

"Two homecoming princesses tearing each other's clothes off." He scoots closer to the action. "Cool."

"Yeah." I turn back to look. "Definitely cool."

## SEVENTEEN

# first dates

* * *

"what are you doing here?"

At about six p.m. on Friday, my father wanders out of his bedroom and finds me curled up in a ball on our family room sofa. My dog, Mogley, is snoring soundly at my feet.

"Watching TV." I flip through the channels, but nothing pops out at me.

"I can see *that*," my dad says. "But why are *you* watching *it here?*"

"Because I *live* here." I know that it shouldn't be this way. I shouldn't be sarcastic. But it is so much easier to give my dad attitude than to admit the real reason why I'm not at Marisol's house, enjoying my usual Friday night rental-movie fest. The REAL REASON is that Marisol sucks. And she has a new boyfriend. And she sold me out for her new *boyfriend* and a $65 ticket to see Coldplay live at the American Airlines Arena.

"Okay . . ." My dad sits next to me on the couch and pats my knee. "What are you going to watch?"

"Why?" I stop channel surfing, surprised to find him somewhat settled on the sofa next to me. "Aren't you going to write tonight?" I ask.

"You know." He sighs. "I don't think so. I've been writing for the last twenty days straight, and I think I've hit a mental roadblock."

"So, you're not going to write?" I repeat.

"No, I'm not." He props his feet up on the coffee table. "Wait." He taps my leg. "Go back to Bravo. That looks interesting."

I turn the TV back to the Bravo channel and set the remote aside. The sofa ripples as my father sinks farther into the cushions. I stare at him watching the TV like I'm witnessing firsthand an alien invasion. When he actually chuckles at the program, I'm nearly convinced that I'm in the middle of a Steven Spielberg film.

"Do you want me to see if there's a movie coming on?" I ask, my heart skipping a beat.

"You know," he smiles over at me, "that would be—"

The sound of our phone ringing prevents him from finishing his sentence. "Let me get that." He gets up to grab the phone in his study. While he's gone, I scroll through the DirecTV menu. There's an Alfred Hitchcock film coming on next at eight p.m. My dad loves Alfred Hitchcock.

"*The Birds* is on at eight," I tell him when he comes back. I scoot my legs closer to my body to make more room for him on the sofa. "Sit down," I say when he keeps standing.

"I'm fine." He stares down at me. "That was Leslie on the phone."

"Yeah, is everything okay?" The way my dad keeps standing there, staring at me, is starting to make me nervous.

"Oh, yes"—he perches on the edge of the sofa—"everything's fine. Leslie called because a friend gave her tickets to the New World Symphony tonight. She wanted to see if I'd like to accompany her."

Leslie was asking my father out on a date? Again?

"What do you think of that idea?" he asks in a neutral voice.

"What do you mean, what do I think of that idea?" I'm not exactly sure what he expects me to say. Does he want me to tell him not to go? Because that's what I think—that he shouldn't go.

"I haven't been to the symphony in years. Not since . . ."

The end of his sentence hangs in the air like the laundry my grandmother puts out to dry. He doesn't have to finish it. I know what he's going to say. He's going to say that he hasn't been to the symphony since my mother died.

"Do you want to go?" It seems like the right question to ask.

"You know"—he runs his fingers through his hair the way he does when he's torn over something—"I'd really like to hear a clarinet tonight, and a bass, and maybe even a piccolo . . . but Alfred Hitchcock—well that's a classic."

"And," I tell him, "You can watch a classic forty times and still get something from it."

My dad gives me an odd look. "Your mom used to say that." He sits on the sofa and stares blankly at the TV. His body is straight. "Maybe I'll tell Leslie no." He stands up and heads for his study.

"Wait." I call him back before I'm even sure what I want to say. "We can always rent *The Birds*."

"Oh . . ." He looks really indecisive. "So I should go?"

I pause. There's no doubt in my mind that I'd rather eat my own toenails than let him go out with Leslie. But I also don't want him to stay here with me out of pity. "You should," I finally say, "do what you really want."

"I think"—he runs his hands through his hair again—"that I would like to go."

"Then go," I tell him.

"I'll go," he says, turning to leave.

I turn back to the TV and start surfing the channels, again. I listen to his phone call through the din of the television.

And even though it hurts to admit it, he sounds excited on the phone, which is great. *Really.* I should be happy for him, I guess.

It's just that his excitement barely matches the excitement I felt a moment ago when for a minute I thought that maybe, just maybe, he might actually have room in his life for me.

that night i wait for leslie and my father to return. in some weird, perverse way I want to witness the end of their date. I want to see if he'll kiss her.

I try to occupy my mind by tearing Leslie apart. It's a hard task because I really, really like Leslie, even if she is totally different from my mom, and I can't understand why my dad is attracted to her.

First, she's agnostic. My mom was a devout Catholic. Secondly, she's completely too topical for my dad. My dad is an intellectual. He reads *The New York Times* and *The Economist*. True, Leslie has a large reading list, but it ranges from *Allure* to *Vanity Fair*.

I pull back my vertical blinds and stare out onto our street. The full moon is beautiful, a perfect white circle tangled up in wispy gray clouds. In the moonlight, our street looks peaceful, and I think about what it's like to have lived here for the last fifteen years. Except for Marc Sanchez being an absolute idiot, it's been really nice.

Across the street, Mr. Middleton is taking his dog Popsicle for a late-night walk. I glance at the clock. Half past one. I wait a little longer, and eventually headlights creep up our street and slowly halt in front of our house. It's them. The silhouette of Leslie's Lincoln Town Car is illuminated by the moon. I move to my second bedroom window, the one that faces into the courtyard of our one-story ranch-style home. I slide the window open just enough so that I can press my ear against the window screen. Then I patiently wait for them to get within hearing distance.

"Thanks for lending me that book," I hear Leslie say, as she passes underneath the archway that leads into the courtyard. She looks over at my window and I wonder if she can see me, but apparently she can't because she says, "Looks like Susie might be asleep already. I hate for us to disturb her. Maybe I should get it later?"

"Susie sleeps like the dead," my dad assures her. "So it's no problem at all."

Leslie hums as she follows my dad up the walkway. "I'm sorry. I can't get that aria out of my head. It was so beautiful."

"Yes," my father says, "yes it was."

"You know"—Leslie steps onto the front porch—"I really thought it was sweet that you held my hand when I cried. That meant a lot to me." Leslie tilts her head up to his.

"It was nice to see that you could be so moved." My dad takes a small step backward.

"So . . ." Leslie says, shifting slightly, "I'll wait here."

"Right." My dad unlocks the door and I hear him enter the house and go into his study. Minutes later he returns with a book in hand. He hands it to Leslie.

"Keep it as long as you like."

"Thanks, I've always wanted to learn more about classical music. This will really help." Leslie brushes her hand across my father's shoulder. They stare at each other for a long time. "I had a really good time."

"I did, too." My dad rocks on his heels. He seems to avoid staring directly at Leslie.

"Do you think you'd like to do it again sometime?" Leslie's voice catches in her throat.

"Yeah, I think so."

"Well"—Leslie inches closer—"give me a call next week. We'll talk."

"Sure." My dad stops rocking. Even though his head is slung low, I can see the tension in his face. Their feet are nearly touching. Leslie leans forward. She rests her head on his chest, and then slowly, very slowly, lets her arms wind up his back and, with her hands, cups his salt-and-pepper hair.

"Joe." She says the word so softly. "Joe."

"Yes . . ." My dad is as stiff as a statue.

"It's okay, Joe," she whispers.

"It's okay?" he repeats, sounding confused.

"Yes." She holds him tightly. "It's okay."

I watch them, unsure of what's happening. His body is still stiff, his hands buried in his pockets. He stares off into the night. I want to go to him. I want to comfort him. I want to tell him that it's not okay. That *I* know.

"No," he says after some time. "I'm not sure that it *is* okay." The minute I hear him speak, I know that he has spoken for both of us.

"Oh. Of course. I understand." Leslie untangles herself from him. "I'll call you, Joe."

"Yeah, okay."

My dad waits until Leslie is safely in her car before coming back into the house. When she's gone, I rest my head on the window ledge and stare into the night. I watch the moon. I try to remember what it looked like the night my mom died. I wonder if it will ever look the same.

# EIGHTEEN

# the mall

. . .

the next day, marisol gets me up at the crack of dawn and drags me to the mall. She's determined to find her homecoming dress and, apparently, to torture me in the process.

For the first hour we're both too sleepy to chat. I'm also a teensy bit annoyed that she sold me out for Ryan Rosenbloom. Occasionally, though, I slip in a question.

"How was the Coldplay concert?" I ask in JCPenney.

"I had the best time," she starts enthusiastically, before suddenly finding herself distracted. "Oh, look, a cute dress."

"Was it just you guys, or did some of his other friends go, too?" I ask two stores and twelve dresses later.

"Um . . . oh, this is nice." She hands me a blue faux cashmere scarf to run my fingers across. "I don't know. It was Ryan and me. Jesse, Ryan's best friend, and Monica, his girlfriend. And another couple—I can't remember their names. Oh, and his cousin Jared, who still doesn't have a date to homecoming."

"Well, tell him good luck with that," I respond dryly.

"You know"—she gives me a look—"Jared is actually pretty cute."

"Like Ryan's cute?" I chuckle under my breath.

"Ryan *is* cute." She gives me a dirty look.

"If that's your type," I mutter.

"He *is* my type," she says, snatching up several pretty thongs from an underwear table.

"Uh-huh," I say in a tone that really says *whatever, retard*. And suddenly, my blood is rushing to my face, turning my cheeks red. I can feel myself gearing up for a knock-down, drag-out fight when suddenly she says, "I'm going to pay for this. If you want to stay here and live in a box all your life, feel free." She stomps off, leaving me pissed off and alone next to a case of padded pink polka-dot push-up bras. And the only thing I can think is: I would have preferred a full-fledged fight. It's a lot fairer than a hit and run.

"you're doing it again," marisol whispers underneath her breath.

On the escalator in Macy's, Marisol decides we're back on speaking terms.

"What?" I hate when she refers to me as if I can't hear her. "What am I doing again?"

"You know," Marisol waves her arm across the span of the escalator. "That weird thing you do when you take like two steps forward and one step back."

That weird thing that she is referring to is the game that I play with escalators. It's like a ritual for me. I can't get on an escalator without doing it. Marisol swears it's my version of an obsessive-compulsive disorder. But I've given it a lot of thought lately, and I think it's more like an affirmation of life. In life, you take strides forward, but you always take a few steps back. But in the end, if you take more steps forward than backward, you're making progress. It also calms my nerves. I try to explain this to Marisol, but she's not buying it.

"Sounds like the best excuse you could think of since the last time we went on an escalator," she tells me.

Which is true. But so what? I'll ride the escalator the way that I ride the escalator. After all, she has her quirks. So what if I've got twenty?

"You know what?" Marisol says when I finally reach the top.

"What?"

"I just realized that you started doing that when we were ten. And that," she mutters under her breath, "is very interesting."

As we walk down the aisle, I run my fingers over all the different fabrics. The seasons are *supposedly* changing and so are the fabrics. Some are cool, some thick and fuzzy, others plain itchy.

"I can't believe it's almost Thanksgiving." Marisol points at a holiday advertisement. "I have to figure out what to buy for Ryan, like, soon because Hanukkah is in three weeks and it's crazy—it's, like, eight days long. Do I give him eight small gifts or do I give him one good one?"

"You're, like, giving each other gifts now?"

"Well . . ." She gives me an irritated look. "Yeah."

"Well . . ." To keep the peace, I adjust my voice so that it's not so sarcastic. "Unless he's giving you eight gifts for Christmas, I'm pretty sure you should just get him one."

"Yeah, you're probably right."

We reach the formal wear department, and, just as I thought, we're surrounded by tacky dresses. It's like stepping into Britney Spears's closet. This is what the excitement is all about?

"So." Marisol ruffles through a rack of puke-brown ball gowns. "I think Ryan is going to invite me to go skiing with his family."

"What, are you guys on hyperspeed?"

"*No* . . . Do you like this?" Marisol holds up a simple, strapless burgundy gown with an empire waist and sheer overlay. And, I hate to say it, it's really beautiful. Instinctively, I touch the fabric. It's silk.

"Yeah, it's nice," I say with one-tenth the excitement I feel.

"I think I'm going to try it on." She sets the dress aside and continues looking. "Anyway, the reason why I'm telling you about the ski trip is that it's the same weekend as"—she pauses, awkwardly—"your mother's memorial service."

November twenty-sixth. The day my mother died. Every year, my father holds a memorial service to keep her memory alive. And every year, the guest list gets shorter and shorter. It's expected, I guess. Sometimes people want to forget. But Marisol? Is this just another one of her ways of telling me that she is ready to move on with her life?

"Are you going to go?" I ask. "I mean, are you going with Ryan?"

"Not if you don't want me to."

And I don't want her to go, but I'm not going to say that because the worst thing in the world is when someone does something out of obligation, not genuine interest. It's like my dad and the symphony all over again. Why can't people make their own decisions and let me feel the way I feel about it?

"Do whatever you want." It's a struggle, but I keep my voice even, unemotional. I examine a terrible taffeta gown in hopes that it'll stop my eyes from glassing over.

"I guess," Marisol says with hesitation, "I'd really like to go."

"Then go," I say coldly. Does she expect me to beg her to stay? "I'm going to try this on." I hurry toward the fitting room. The minute I shut the door, I start to cry.


it takes exactly ten minutes for a sales clerk to knock on the stall door.

I don't answer her right away. It's not that I'm trying to be difficult, but the only sound that will leave my mouth is the sound of me gasping. That's how I sound when I cry hard.

"Hello? Sweetie, are you okay?" Her gentle tap turns into a persistent knock. She's probably baffled as to why I picked her fitting room to have a nervous breakdown.

"Miss"—her key turns the lock—"if you don't respond, I'm going to have to come in." And sure enough, two seconds later, she's standing in front of me, motherly concern written all across her tan face.

I know to her I probably look a mess. My face is streaked black from my not-so-waterproof waterproof mascara. My hair is stuck to my face in patches of unruly curls. And to add to that, I'm sitting on a tattered stool, wearing the terrible taffeta gown, which is even more terrible because it is too tight for my hips and too big for my boobs.

"Oh, honey." The fitting room attendant digs into her pocket and hands me a crumpled tissue. "The dress isn't that bad. I can get one for you in your size."

"I'm fine, really." My voice is wobbly. I clear my throat. "I'm fine," I repeat. But I accept the tissue and blow into it something fierce.

"Tell me, it's the gown. Isn't it?" The attendant kneels down and pushes the hair away from my face.

I shake my head no and proceed to choke on my own boogers.

"Oh." The attendant smiles sympathetically. "It's a boy?"

Again, I shake my head.

"Well . . ." She seems to ponder her remaining options. "Did you have a fight with a friend?"

I nod yes, blowing my nose in the already soggy tissue. She's super-perceptive, I think.

"Do you want to talk about it?" she asks gently.

What was there to talk about? The only thing I know for sure is that inside I feel like a complete mess. And that realization starts a fresh wave of tears.

"Sweetie . . ." The attendant shuts the door behind her and locks it. "Now wait. I know things are bad for you right now, but you've got to pull yourself together. You'll work this out. Friendships"—she lifts my chin so that I look directly into her brown eyes—"are the most important thing you can have in your life. Sometimes they have their ups and downs. Sometimes it's your fault and sometimes it's not. But the key to handling those ups and downs is to remember that good friends will always find their way back to each other. Understand?"

I nod. Through my tears, I admire her kind face. When she smiles at me, laugh lines crease the sides of her cheeks.

"I'm just being a crybaby." I wipe my nose with a new tissue she offers me.

"There's nothing wrong with a good cry. But"—she considers my outfit with such disdain, I can't help but laugh—"there is something terribly wrong with that dress. What can we do to fix it?"

I shrug my shoulders. Doesn't she know there's nothing that can be done about the way I look?

"I know." She slaps her hand on her thigh. "I'll be back."

thirty minutes later, i emerge from the ladies' fitting room tear-free and, thanks to Jeanette, the overly perceptive sales clerk, wearing the coolest pair of Bubblegum jeans ever to be seen and a simple black tank with small embroidered butterflies running down the left side and a double-wide sea-green belt that hangs perfectly over my wide hips. I look . . . God, it's like impossible to believe, but I look so . . . normal.

Now, if I can only find Marisol. I haven't seen her since I went into the fitting room. And she doesn't appear to be anywhere nearby. This, I think as I try to tear myself away from the mirror, is why I need a cell phone. And that's when I hear IT.

"No way."

Or, should I say HER? It can't be . . .

But there she is. A thousand watts of sheer constipation frozen on her face.

"Hi, Tamara." I force a huge grin. Homecoming or not, I look great, and I'm not about to let Tamara's sour expression ruin my high. "Hi, Mrs. Cruz." I wield my false smile at Tamara's mother.

"What happened to you?" Tamara voice drips with disbelief.

"Tamara, really." Mrs. Cruz gives Tamara a sharp look. "You look so stylish, Susie. Did you have a makeover?"

"Not really." I glance over my shoulder to make sure Jeanette is nowhere near. "I just, you know, was doing a little bit of shopping and found this. I decided to wear it home."

It's a little white lie—I know. But so what? It's obvious that I had somewhat of a makeover. But I'm not about to admit that to the mother of the homecoming princess from hell. Especially, after the HCPFH stole my . . .

What exactly did Tamara *steal* from me?

Whatever. The look of disbelief on Tamara's face—the one that says I might possibly be a threat to her and her future happiness with Danny—is worth a zillion lies, if you ask me.

"Doesn't she look great, Tamara?"

"Yeah." Tamara rolls her eyes. "Great."

Mrs. Cruz smiles at me, unaware (as always) of Tamara's attitude. "It's a funny thing that we should run into you like this. I was just asking Tamara how you were doing. I haven't seen you since your mother's memorial service last year."

"Right, I remember." Every year Tamara and her parents come to my mother's memorial service. I never really minded their attending. The truth is I barely noticed they were there, except sometimes when I thought that Tamara was lucky to still have a mother. But this year, I'm not sure I can stand the idea of Tamara standing in my house, flaunting her very much alive mother and her souvenir homecoming keychain.

"Well, we really should get back to our shopping. Tamara's looking for a *new* homecoming dress." Mrs. Cruz sighs. "Apparently, the other one wasn't the right color. Have you found your dress yet?"

"No." My eyes shift to Tamara. She's absolutely gloating. I almost wished that I had Jessica here to slap her. "Actually," my eyes drift to the floor. "I'm not going."

"Oh. Well, that's too bad. Yes, well we're off to find a red dress. Red dress, can you believe it?" Mrs. Cruz rolls her eyes at Tamara.

"It's Danny's favorite color," Tamara pipes in. "Did you know that?"

I can hear the challenge in her voice.

"No," I say, rather slowly, "I didn't. But"—my palms feel shaky, and I can't believe that I'm going to say what I'm about to say, but I say it anyway—"that might explain why I saw Jessica here earlier, desperately looking for one."

"What?" Tamara hisses, swinging her head around, scanning the crowd for Jessica's huge breasts and glossy black hair. "You're kidding, right?"

It's another white lie, I know. But still, it's so much fun to turn the tables on Tamara that I don't bother to answer her question. Instead, I muster up a smile for Mrs. Cruz and say: "It's nice seeing you, Mrs. Cruz."

"You, too, Susie," Mrs. Cruz says, turning to follow Tamara, who is frantically searching for Jessica, like she might be hiding under a table, holding all the red dresses hostage. "We'll see you in a few weeks at the memorial service."

"Right." A few weeks until my mother's memorial service—like I could ever forget.

# NINETEEN

# interlude

· · ·

on the ride home from the mall, i do my best to ignore my father. He's pretty much number one on my crap list, followed by:

1. Marisol—Apparently, she left me at the mall.

2. Leslie—Apparently, she wants to get down my father's pants.

3. Danny—Apparently, I'm not good enough for him when über-bitches like Tamara and Jessica are.

4. Tamara and Jessica—They're just evil. What other explanation is needed?

Unfortunately, my father fails to take the hint that my jutted shoulder, brooding lips, and need to blare the radio past human comprehension are actually all part of an effort to drown him out.

"Did something happen with Marisol?" he asks for the fifth time since we hit Kendall Drive. "Why did she leave you behind?"

"Still don't want to talk about it, Dad." I stare out the window and watch the world pass by. Miami is so large and crowded. I remember ten years ago when the houses still had yards. Now it seems like every house is just two breaths away from its neighbor. The closeness can make you feel claustrophobic.

"Susie, is this about last night . . . ?" The light turns green, and one second later someone is beeping their horn.

"Nothing ever changes in Miami," I mumble under my breath.

"What did you say?" My dad leans toward me.

"Nothing," I mumble again.

"Susie, look, I know that it's weird for you that Leslie and I are . . . hanging out. It's weird for me, too, but—"

"Dad, I don't want to talk about that either!" I roll down my window all the way. Right now, I can use the fresh air.

"Fine, but we're going to have to talk about it eventually. The sooner the better. Okay?"

I let the question dissipate. All around me cars are moving. People are traveling toward their next destination, but in this car with my dad, I feel like my next destination is nowhere.

I try to focus on counting the landmarks that we pass. I start with Baptist Hospital on my left and then add Tony Roma's to my right. Next to Tony Roma's is an old, run-down porn shop. What kind of people shop there? Probably pervs, I think.

"What day is it?" I ask.

"Um, November twelfth."

"Next weekend's homecoming," I tell him.

"Are you going?"

"Nope. Apparently, I'm not pretty enough to be asked."

"What? Oh, Susie. Are you upset with your new clothes? I think you look great."

I shake my head at him. He still doesn't get it. Even with my stylish new look, I'm still only average. Except now, I'm normal-looking average. I'm fitting-in average.

"Susie," he says, realizing that he's not reaching me. "It's not true. You know that's not true. Right?"

"Yeah, Dad." I say with false cheer. "I know." I stick my head out the window and close my eyes. The wind whips across my face and stings me. The corners of my eyes burn, and my pent-up tears begin to fall.

But that's okay. Because no one can see me cry.

# loneliness

· · ·

i don't go to school monday or tuesday. i tell my father that I'm sick. I'm not sure if he buys my poor Ferris Bueller impression (I coughed until my throat was sore and littered my room with dry, crumpled-up tissues) or if I'm still riding the waves of his guilt train, but he doesn't argue with me about my prognosis. When I tell him that I have the flu, he nods his head and hands me the remote to my TV.

For two days, I stay in my bed. I don't move. I don't shower. I leave my bedroom only when I have to pee. Other than that, I wrap myself in my covers, turn on my side, and spend hours watching television. Television is a great escape for me. It's the only time I can actually be awake and mentally asleep.

On Monday, I watch *Maury Povich, Montel,* even old reruns of *Jerry Springer,* and I feel a little better about myself and my situation. By the end of day one, I've convinced myself that there is a whole world full of losers that are way worse off than me.

In the afternoon, I watch the soaps. I check out *Days of Our Lives, The Young and the Restless,* and *All My Children.* To my surprise, I'm pretty current with the story lines. It seems the plots haven't really progressed that much since the last time I was sick three years ago.

I spend Tuesday reading to the point of exhaustion. When I drift off to sleep, I dream that I'm a guest on *Tyra*. It's one of those episodes where you admit to having a secret crush on someone you went to high school with, but I'm Tyra's only guest. I sit onstage surrounded by empty chairs. When I look at the audience, all I see are classmates and teachers. Mr. Murphy sits in the front row and waves at me. He mouths to me, *Sit up straight. Don't slouch.* Jessica and Tamara sit in the back with Billy Wilson. They shout out "Geek!" whenever the cameras stop rolling. Marisol sits in the front row, talking to her mother on a cell phone.

Danny's sits behind a translucent screen. I watch his silhouette, but he never comes out to see me. Tyra calls his name over and over again, but he never comes out from behind the screen.

tuesday afternoon when my dad comes home from work, he finds me staring at the wall. I've run out of reading material, and I'm afraid if I fall asleep I might find myself in some parallel *Tyra* universe.

"Hey." He sets up a tray on my bed, and before I turn to look at him, I already know what he's brought for me. It's a ritual my dad started after my mom died: hot wonton soup and a milky-white bag filled with fortune cookies. When I was a little girl, whenever I got sick my mom used to make homemade chicken soup. I guess my dad figured Chinese was the next best thing.

"Hey." I sit up and clean the crud out of my eyes. My hair feels like a frizzy ball resting precariously on the top of my head. My gown is damp against my skin. I feel the prickle of armpit hair underneath the flap of my arm. It's official. I stink.

"I brought you soup, and of course"—he dangles the milky bag in front of me—"your fortune."

"Thanks, Dad." I place the bag on the tray, next to the pint of soup. I don't eat right away. Thanks to my nerves, my appetite is practically nil.

"Not hungry?" My dad opens the soup, and stirs it with the plastic spork. The aroma wafts up through the air and clings to my nostrils.

"A little, I guess. But it's too hot right now." I point toward the rising steam as confirmation.

"Oh." He stands up and walks over to my window. He pulls on the cord of the blinds and light floods the room. "That's a little better. Cheerier. So . . ." He claps his hands together and smiles. I can tell that he's trying really hard, and that breaks my heart just a little. "Think you'll be ready to go back to school tomorrow?" There's so much hope in his eyes that all my thoughts of prolonging my illness to the end of the week disappear.

"Yeah, Dad, I feel a little better." The truth is I am fine. Beside my frizzy hair and stinky armpits, I am perfect on the outside. But on the inside, I'm a wreck. But how do you say that to your dad? "No, I'm feeling a lot better."

"You know, Leslie told me that Marisol seems a little down, too. Did you have a fight?"

"What, do you and Leslie talk on the phone every day now?" I ask him in a flat voice.

"Not every day, but we do talk occasionally. Does that bother you?"

"Does that bother me? I don't know, Dad. What do you think?" I give him a dead stare. If he doesn't get that his dating my best friend's mother BOTHERS me, then I'm not going to BOTHER to explain it to him.

"Okay, um . . ." He rubs his temples. "You know I wouldn't do anything to intentionally hurt you."

"No, I know you wouldn't do anything *intentionally* to hurt me."

"That's not fair."

"Well, Dad, like you've told me before, life isn't always fair."

I watch his face sag, like the skin of a cut-open tomato. I suck in the air around me. I'm angry, not sad. I'm angry that he's dating someone else and that he's forgotten about my mother, about chicken soup, about driving to Sears after church every Sunday. I'm angry that he's ready to move on and for what? For some therapist who's so insecure she has to constantly ask her daughter how she looks?

"Maybe we should talk about this later." My dad retreats to the door. He looks broken. His shoulders are slumped. The space around his eyes is wrinkled with tension.

"Everything is always later." I tell him with a smile. "Right, Dad? Right?"

"Susie—" His voice is dangerously thin. "We'll talk about this later."

He holds my gaze for a second before he firmly shuts the door behind him. After he's gone, I debate what I said, and what I could have said to make him stay. I think about screaming after him, anything to make him hear me. But in the end, I do nothing, because I know it's no use. What's the point in yelling words that have already been left behind?

# TWENTY-ONE

# apologies

. . .

the next few days pass in a blur. i walk through the halls. i eat my lunch. I attend classes. I don't smile. I don't talk. I don't interact with anyone, but maybe nobody notices because for me that's pretty normal.

Wednesday Danny cancels his tutoring session. He tells me that he has to meet with Tamara and a group of her friends to finish their homecoming plans. I imagine them all sitting around Denny's debating limousines over Hummers, a suite at the Sofitel or a room at Loews on the beach. I tell myself I don't care. I tell myself that I don't want to rip Tamara's freshly highlighted hair from her head during driver's ed, and that when I ignored her stupid student council story, I might have actually hurt her feelings.

On the night of homecoming, I hide out at home, under my covers. I keep my cordless phone next to me. I don't anticipate that the phone will ring. But for whatever reason, in the back of my mind, I hope that Marisol will call me to tell me something—anything. But she doesn't.

I haven't spoken to Marisol since the mall. Not a word, not even when I ran into her at our locker. To be honest, I'm hurt but impressed. Marisol's never been able to give me the silent treatment for more than four days. She would always tell me to talk to her and express my feelings. But this week, she's been different. Tougher.

To survive our separation, I tell myself that I'm stronger. Anything she can do, I can do better. But that may not be true. I've dialed her number three times tonight, but I hung up the phone before it could ring.

And then I gave myself the pep talk. I told myself that she deserves for me to be mad at her. How could she abandon me . . . for a boy? How could she want our parents to date? She's in the wrong. What right does she have to be mad at me?

It's been surprisingly easy to be angry at Marisol, primarily because she's so happy. When I went back to school on Wednesday, she was wearing lip gloss and her hair was slicked back into a ponytail. She looked like she had just stepped out of a Noxzema commercial—fresh and excited. Worse, she was eating lunch with Ryan. She sat at his table with HIS friends. She smiled and talked to everyone like SHE belonged. With THEM.

So I guess I shouldn't be surprised that she hasn't called me today. And that she didn't call me yesterday or the day before. And that she may never call me again.

When the clock turns eight, I crawl out from under the covers and tread into the kitchen. My dad is gone for the night. I didn't ask him where he was going, and he didn't bother to tell me. So tonight it's just me and Mogley.

I open the refrigerator and step into the light. I feel like I could eat the world, but I decide to settle for a Snapple and a yogurt. I take it outside into the fresh air. I love late November. Miami is beautiful in late November. The wind trickles in from the Atlantic and the sweltering heat finally breaks and, for a minute, autumn exists. But just for a minute.

I light a candle and inhale the scent of my backyard. It smells like freshly cut grass, which is one reason why my backyard is different from most backyards in Miami. It doesn't have a pool or an overhead screen. It's a simple garden that my mother planted ten years ago. And I love it. I love it so much that I've single-handedly kept it up since she died.

I sit on the patio swing and rock back and forth under the moon. I feel calm. And that feels strange.

I sip my Snapple and stare at the sky. My mom and I used to do this a lot. I'd rest my head on her belly. We'd hold hands and talk about "secrets of the earth." Or at least that's what she called it. I think she was trying to be mysterious for the benefit of my little ears.

*"Why are there so many stars, Mommy?"*

*"I don't know, sweetie; I think God just wanted us to know that we're not alone."*

*"But we're not alone. We've got Daddy."*

*"Yes, but sometimes you can be surrounded by people and still feel very alone. Understand?"*

*"No."*

*"Well, one day you will."*

I close my eyes, and relive other moments with my mom, like that time I was five and I peed in the middle of Wal-Mart and she nearly died of embarrassment. Or when I got sick in the second grade and had to be taken to the hospital to have tests run. I was really scared. I think about my mom's graduation from nursing school. I think about the birthday party I had when I was eight. I wonder what she would have said to me when I got my period. Would she have been like my father and tossed a box of maxi pads at me, then scurried away? Or would she have sat me down and talked to me? What would she have told me on those days?

And then I ask myself if a day has gone by that I haven't thought about her.

When she died, I told myself that I would think about her every day, but I haven't, not because I don't love her, but mostly because it's too hard to think about her and live. When I do think about her, I think about how she must have felt during those last few moments of her life. I wonder if she was scared or if she thought about my father and me. I wonder if she knew she was going to die or if she thought that she would survive. I wonder if people have a real comprehension of their own mortality.

The neighborhood is unusually silent except for the sound of a guitar being played. The melody ripples across the distance and pools at my feet. It takes me a while to figure out where it is coming from, but soon I realize that the sound is coming from the back of Marc's house.

I prop myself up and glance into his backyard. I can see his patio clearly. The light is on and he is sitting there, alone, playing the guitar. I haven't heard him play the guitar since we were nine. Our parents used to make us take lessons together. He hated it. I loved it. I had no idea he kept up with it. He actually sounds decent, though a little choppy on certain parts of the bridge.

"Marc, we're leaving now." Mrs. Sanchez's voice drifts through the waist-high mesh fence. I hear her heels and subconsciously straighten my spine and try to stop breathing. It's not that I don't like her. It's just that she's real intimidating. She's super-tall, and her stare is always condescending. I don't know how my mom was ever friends with her, but my mom always did have a way of bonding with people, even the snottiest adults.

"Are you sure you're going to be okay? Because your father and I can stay—"

"Mom, it's fine." His voice is harsh, and it reminds me of the way that I spoke to my father earlier this week. The guitar stops. I lean back on the swing. I'm having a hard time not watching.

"Marc, it's going to take time, but once that time passes you will be better than fine, you'll be great. Okay?" She crosses the space between them with two long strides. "I love you."

"Uh-huh."

"Marc," she sighs, obviously hurt. "Okay. Be good." She turns—then stops and stares into my yard, at my candle still burning on the table adjacent to me. "Oh. Hi, Susie."

"Oh . . . Hi, Mrs. Sanchez." I slide to the left of the burning candle, try to hide even though there's no point in hiding now.

"I didn't see you sitting there. How's your father?"

"Me either," Marc says sarcastically. He turns in his chair and gives me a look.

"Marc," Mrs. Sanchez reprimands him, which only makes me feel worse. "Susie, how's your father?"

"He's fine, Mrs. Sanchez."

"Where's he at? In the house working on his book?" She glances at her watch, impatient like always.

"No, he's out." I try not to waste her time with lengthy answers.

"Well, tell him I said hi. And that we'll talk about your mom's memorial service next week. Okay?"

"Okay."

"Bye, now. And you," she turns back to Marc, "be good." Then she *clickety-click*s away.

With Mrs. Sanchez gone, I find myself in an awkward position. There is a tiny moment when I actually consider saying something, but in situations where you're caught spying on your neighbor, there are minimal possibilities for conversation restarters.

I contemplate extinguishing my candle and slinking ever so slowly back into my house. But I'm really tired of letting Marc chase me away. I'm really tired of letting everyone chase me away.

"How long you been there?" Marc asks.

"What?" My voice is prickly.

"How long have you been listening to me?"

"I haven't been listening to anything that sounded like anything." It's a dig. I know.

"I was just trying something new," he says reflectively.

"Well, it doesn't go like that," I tell him pointedly.

"You still play?"

I let the question hang out there because the real question is, why is Marc even bothering to talk to me?

"Well, do you?"

"Yeah," I say, thinking about how much older he sounds since the last time we had an actual conversation. "I play. You've never heard me?" It's a trick question. Anyone who lives in the neighborhood knows that I play. I play in my garden all the time, mostly on Sunday afternoons when Marisol comes over to do her homework. In my mother's garden I'm safe. No one—not even Marc Sanchez—can take that away from me.

"Yeah, I guess I've heard you. You've gotten really good."

The compliment is hard to take because it comes from Marc. A few nice words can't erase the last six years.

"My girlfriend broke up with me tonight."

So typical. Marc's having a pity party, and by process of elimination and proximity I'm *allowed* to be his only guest.

"Ugh, this sucks, this really, really sucks. I really liked that chick, you know?"

I stay silent. I don't care that Marc's silly, slutty girlfriend broke up with him. I don't care that he's having a bad night. I've got my own problems to think about.

Unfortunately, the longer I stay silent, the longer he keeps talking.

"Man, I don't know. It was like everything was going great, you know? And I . . . we were cool together. She's pretty and funny and popular. We just . . . it was like great. And then she dumps me tonight.

We were supposed to go to this dumb dance together, and she dumps me. She says that I didn't *really* want to go to the dance with her. And that I make everything hard. And that we like different things. And that her mom says that compatibility is super-important . . . That's why her parents divorced, you know, because they were *incompatible*. And that"—his voice rises—"is why she thinks we're no good together. And *she*, get this fucking shit, doesn't want to waste any more time with someone who's not her match." He picks up a rock and throws it hard at the side of his house.

"Well, did you?" I ask, even though I'm thinking that I shouldn't have asked anything, because at the very end of his *my life sucks* monologue, his voice actually cracked, and I'm seriously afraid that he might start to cry.

"Huh?"

"Did you not want to go to homecoming?"

His patio light flicks off, which makes me think that I was right about the crying thing. I can't see him, but I hear him sigh exceptionally loud. Then I hear the grass crunch underfoot.

"Hey." He stops a few feet from my chair.

"Do you do that a lot?" I ask him, even though I know he doesn't. But sometimes you have to say something just because.

"What?"

"Jump my fence?"

"No."

"Oh."

"You mind?" He pulls out a pack of cigarettes and lights one with my candle. He motions with his head for permission to sit across from me. I shrug my shoulders and he sits down.

"This dance thing is stupid. Who goes to dances? It's so gay." He takes a drag from his cigarette and holds it out to me.

"No thanks. So you did give her a hard time?" I sit up and study

112

his silhouette in the dark. I find the fact that he's sitting across from me after all these years . . . uncomfortable.

"If I gave her a hard time, do you think that I would be wearing this stupid tuxedo thing?"

"That's a tux?" All I can make out in the dark is a white shirt and a dark pair of pants.

"Well, part of it. I took off the tie and jacket after she left." He tugs at the collar and scratches his neck. "It felt weird. It's gross how other people wear these things before you do."

"Yeah, well, try wearing a thong."

"What?" The end of his cigarette burns orange. "What does that have to do with anything?"

"A thong? An invention designed for the sheer purpose of putting women back in bondage."

Marc gives me a blank look.

"Forget it."

"So what are you doing out here on a Saturday night?"

"I don't know," I mumble. I'd rather not get into my abandonment issues right now.

"Usually, I go out with Sheila on Saturday. She likes to go to the movies and then she likes to go to Dairy Queen." He lets out a rumbling moan. "Man!"

"Wow. You act like this is the end of the world. She's just a chick. Hey—" I pause to explain because he looks like he's about to snap my head off. "Your word, not mine."

He takes another drag off his cigarette. And I wonder if one day he'll get lung cancer and die. I know, it's an evil thing to think. But as he flicks the butt of his cigarette into MY garden and lights another one, the thought feels justified.

"So you're friends with Danny Diaz now?"

"What are you talking about?"

"I've seen you guys hanging around after school together."

"Oh." So this is another part of the reason why he can stand to talk to me?

"You know Danny?" I raise my eyebrows. I've never seen Danny speak to Marc. I can't imagine them as friends.

"I know of him. I have his sister, Dalia, in my biology class. She's hot. You know? Well, she . . ." Blah, blah, blah, and Marc continues to talk, but, for some reason, I stop listening. His mouth moves, but the words that come out sound like mush.

"So what do you think?"

I shrug and turn my face away. I think about all the crap he's put me through since elementary school—the way he stopped talking to me, the way he made me disappear—and how, after all this time, he can sit across from me and blab total nonsense without feeling like he remotely owes me any type of explanation. What kind of person does that?

"I'm sorry," he says. "I'm running on and on. I do that when I get . . . weird."

"Weird?" I repeat, even though I'm silently rehashing every single snub that has taken place since the fifth grade.

"Not weird, not like that." He shakes his head, and puffs his cigarette. "You know, I really am sorry."

I turn to look at him. He inhales deeply and holds the smoke inside. His head falls forward, and his face is concealed in the shadows. He's like a poster boy for love gone wrong, and the crappy thing is that I'm actually starting to feel sorry for him.

"Look, Marc . . ." I blow out my candle and stand. "We all mess up. Believe me. Talk to Sheila. Apologize. Get over it. I don't care. I'm going inside."

I turn to leave, but Marc grabs my arm and holds me in place.

"Wait—" he says, his grip firm.

"Hey—" I try to shrug free, but he holds on tighter.

"That's not what I'm trying to apologize for right now, you know?" He stares at me as if I'm supposed to understand whatever it is he's fumbling toward. But all I want is for him to let go of my arm.

"Marc, let go."

"I'm sorry," he says, ignoring me. "That's all. I . . . wow." Marc stands. The cigarette falls to the floor. He pushes it out with the corner of his patent-leather rental shoe. The whole time, he never lets my arm go. "I never thought we'd ever talk again. You know?"

I stay quiet. It's my thing.

"I thought that we'd hate each other for the rest of our lives, and then, I guess, tonight, I don't know what, but I'm sorry, okay?" The last part comes out as a whisper, and I remember when Marc and I were seven and playing in his tree house. By mistake he nudged me over the side, and when I landed on my back on the grass below, he put his hand over my mouth to muffle my cries while he kept telling me that he was sorry in that same little voice. The only difference (besides the fact that he nearly suffocated me) was that he also kept begging me to not tell my mother.

"Marc"—although I'd rather not have this conversation, I have to ask—"what are you sorry for?"

"I'm sorry"—Marc pauses, long enough to let go of my arm—"about everything that happened after your mom and stuff."

"Oh, Marc, I don't wanna talk about this—" Not now, not ever.

"But I do. Susie, if I don't, I'll just feel like a chickenshit tomorrow. I mean, I'm already a chickenshit. If I weren't chickenshit, I'd be at that stupid dance with Sheila. Yeah, it's gay, but so what?" He shakes his head, turns from me, and runs his free hand through his hair.

Oh, the irony.

"Marc?" My voice is wobbly.

"Yeah?"

"I'm chickenshit, too."

I think about Marisol. I let the whole week pass without apologizing to her. And now she's out having the first Cinderella night of her life, and I'm stuck here like an idiot with my jerk-off neighbor who isn't so bad. I guess.

"This week's been hard for me, too," I admit.

We lapse into silence. I feel jumbled.

"So, I guess we're both chickenshit," Marc says finally. He sits down next to me on my swing. "You know, I really am sorry about your mom and stuff."

"Marc, please—"

"No. After your mom died, I really didn't know what to say, or how to be around you, and I was a really bad friend, and I'm sorry."

He speaks in his tiny voice, but this time it catches in his throat and stays stuck. I know that he's crying. I just know. Because I know Marc. Marc is sensitive. I don't know why the last six years made me forget that.

"Okay, Marc." I don't know what else to do, so I put my arm stiffly around his shoulder. Gradually my other arm finds its way around his back. "It's okay."

It's funny how Marc, my first enemy, should become the first boy that I hold. But life, I can hear my mom say, is funny like that. I look around the garden and exhale. It is the first cry that I have had all week where I don't feel completely alone.

# TWENTY-TWO

# amends

. . .

at two fifteen a.m. i call marisol's private phone line. i figure by now she should be home, tucked in bed, watching Nick at Nite. So I almost hang up the phone when she answers it half asleep.

"Marisol?" Despite my two-hour pep talk, my voice is tentative.

"Yeah? Who's this?"

Of course, I know that she knows it's me. Of course, I know that she's trying to be cold. But still, I give her the benefit of the doubt. "It's me, Susie."

"Yeah," Marisol says, sounding resigned. "I know. What do you want?"

So much for the benefit of the doubt.

"Were you sleeping?" I ask stupidly. Obviously she was sleeping.

"Uh-huh."

"Okay . . ." I lose my nerve, and, for me, apologies require massive doses of nerve. "I'll call you tomorrow."

"No, you woke me up. Just tell me what you want."

The problem with Marisol is that she's always pretty good at calling people out. She likes follow-through, even if it means stumbling through the worst part of it.

"Well, the thing is . . . ThethingisI'msorry." I say it in one breath because I'm honestly afraid that if I don't, I never will.

"You're what?" Marisol's voice is softer now.

"I'm sorry," I tell her again, only this time the words don't run together, and I take a deep breath to continue the thought. "I'm sorry if I made you feel bad for having a date to homecoming. I didn't mean to. I mean . . . I guess, in my own way, I was jealous, and a little bit insecure, and afraid that I was going to lose you."

Once the words start, they flow. I think on some subconscious level I've been analyzing this fight for the better part of the week, especially during those moments watching *Tyra*.

"Susie, what would make you think that you were going to lose me?" Leave it to Marisol to get to the point.

"Not lose you entirely," I say quickly, "but lose out on doing stuff with you. I don't want to be the third wheel on a Friday night. I don't want for us not to have our movie night, or hang out on Halloween . . . I don't want to lose that." I try to sniffle quietly. I'm crying. How stupid is that? I keep telling myself that this week shouldn't have been so hard for me. But it has been.

"Susie, maybe—and I'm not saying that's going to happen with this guy—but maybe, just maybe, we're not going to be able to spend so much time together when we're older, but would that be such a bad thing? Think about it. It'll give us more to talk to each other about. Right?"

"Uh-huh." I brush the tears away with the back of my hand. They're sliding like puddles down my cheeks.

"You're like my sister. You're never going to lose that. I will never let any guy come between that. 'Kay?"

"Yeah," I whisper into the phone. "But what about my mother's memorial service?" I ask.

"I'm not going skiing," she says. "I made that decision before you called me. I'm sorry that I even asked you."

"Oh." On some level my heart heals just a little.

"Good. Do you want to get a tissue or something?" Marisol asks gently.

"How do you know I'm crying?" I half hiccup, half giggle into the phone.

"Because, I know you." We laugh together, and I take a moment to cherish how right it feels.

"Hold on." I pad quietly down the hall to the bathroom and swipe a roll of toilet paper. Then I pad back to my room, sit on my bed, and wrap my comforter around me. "Okay, I have a whole roll of toilet paper. Tell me everything." I tuck my knees under my chin and rest my head against the wall. "And when you're done, I'm going to tell you everything that happened to me tonight, and I'll give you a clue right now—Marc Sanchez."

"No," Marisol shrieks. "Hey, but wait, I go first."

"Okay," I tell her, suddenly filled with love for her. "You go first."

# TWENTY-THREE

# la casa diaz, part ii

· · ·

the next day i am surprisingly calm. i get up. i brush my teeth. I take a shower. I play my guitar. I do homework. I am perfectly normal until my father drops me off in front of Danny Diaz's house. It is only then, right before I reach to ring the doorbell, that I have a mini–panic attack. All I know is that I suddenly feel insecure about almost every part of my body. I feel like my clothes are too casual and my hair is out of place. And what if Danny has forgotten that I was invited to dinner? What if I'm showing up and nobody is home?

I glance at their driveway. Three cars are in it. They are definitely home.

Part of the problem is that I've straightened my hair and I'm wearing the outfit from the mall. I look better, but I don't feel like me. I don't feel like me at all.

Which, Marisol told me while she straightened my hair and dabbed cream eye shadow on my eyelids, was the point.

Not that being me is a bad thing, but feeling like me—the insecure me—definitely is a problem.

Okay, I can do this.

I push my finger forward and slide it across the doorbell's soft center. One little move and the whole house will know that I'm here. *Okay, do it. Do it.* But I can't. My hand falls limply back to my side. If I can't ring the doorbell, how will I make it through dinner?

I take two small steps backward, and then, with the grace of a dancer, turn silently on my heels and run smack into Danny.

"Going somewhere?"

His smile lets me know that he's been standing behind me for a good while.

"No," I tell him. "I wasn't going anywhere."

"Then what were you doing?" he asks.

"Um." I search high and low for an excuse. It's not like I can say that I left my purse in my car. My dad dropped me off, and my purse is hanging across my shoulder. "Um," I repeat.

"'Um,'" Danny mimics.

"Well," I stall, "the thing is"—and that's when the best of the worst lies that I can think of comes tumbling out of my mouth— "The thing is that I have mud on my shoes and I wanted to get it off . . . in the grass." I point to the grass as if it should be perfectly obvious to him that that was what I was about to do before I bumped into him.

"Your shoes look fine." He stares down at my spotless sandals. They're brown leather without a speck of dirt on them.

"It's on the bottom." I sidestep him and head for the lawn, where I avidly rub my feet on the grass.

I can tell that he's not buying my lame excuse, but he still says, "Okay, Susie. I think that's crazy, but okay." And then he pulls on the side of my shirt playfully. It's not the first time he's touched me, but it feels as if it might as well be. My skin feels hot and tingly. "We should go inside."

He cuts up the path, and I follow him. He rubs his finger over the doorbell and turns to wink at me. He's teasing me, and I like it. "My mom was really excited about your coming today." He tells me over his shoulder. "She made Dalia and me clean for like four hours."

"No way." I'm pretty sure that he's teasing me again. But what if he's not?

"It's okay. We have to clean during the weekends anyway. My mom thinks that a family that cleans together stays together. Actually, she makes us do most of the cleaning." Danny slides through the doorway, and I follow.

"Why do you have to do all the work?" I ask.

"Because." Danny shakes his head at me, like the concept of family is foreign to me, which, maybe it is. "She and my dad pay all the bills. It's fair to me. Besides, my mom says that if we think we're too grown-up to clean the house, then we must be old enough to get a job. And with soccer practice, I don't have time to work, so I'm absolutely happy to clean my room, vacuum the living room, do the laundry, and dust." Danny runs his fingers through his hair and my toes tingle. He's heart-wrenchingly cute today.

"Wow, you really do clean." I try not to look at his lips. But my eyes are drawn to them. It's like ever since I've given myself permission to like him, I can't help but notice everything and anything about him.

"Don't you?" We enter the kitchen, and the scent of Pine-Sol and onions permeates the air. Danny takes a seat on one of the three bar stools crowded around the kitchen counter. I stand next to him.

"No, we have a maid that comes three times a week."

"That must be the life to live."

"Not really; she always forgets to clean the bathroom and then I have to do it, which sucks." I run my hand over the countertop.

I feel really, really strange.

"Susie?" Danny's voice dips a little.

"Huh?" I smile at him without thinking.

"Why do you keep staring at my lips?"

"Huh?" My cheeks burn red.

"Do I have something in my teeth?" Danny smiles widely and twists his head to the side. He leans in really closely. His breath smells like ripe oranges.

"No," I look down, and my hair drifts into my face. I wish the floor would open up, and I would be sucked under. I'm afraid that if I look up, my eyes will be drawn back to his lips. . . . "There's nothing in your teeth."

"Why don't you sit here?" Danny pulls out the bar stool next to his and pushes it closer to him, leaving only a foot of space in between. When I hesitate, he taps the seat expectantly. Reluctantly, I accept his offer. And before I know it, we're sitting knee to knee staring at each other.

"Where's everyone else?" I ask him. The house is so silent.

"Oh, my mom forgot the Cuban bread and *tres leches*, so she and my dad ran back out to get it. Dalia is at her boyfriend's house. They got into a fight last night at homecoming, so she'll be over there kissing his butt for a while. And *mi abuelo* is outside talking to the ducks. So . . ." His voice trails off.

"So . . ." I repeat, watching him. He's staring at me like he's considering my face.

"I like your hair like that. Straight." He leans forward and passes his fingertips over a strand of stray hair before brushing it behind my ear. "It's really soft."

His breath is hot on my face. His glance is unnerving. The tingling sensation returns quickly and glides down my belly over my thighs and settles behind my kneecaps. They feel weak, and I'm thankful that I have the stool to support my wobbly body. I'm mesmerized by him, by how a single touch from him can make me feel sexy. I've never felt sexy in my life. Before this moment, I would have never known how to describe what that word truly means. But now with Danny Diaz's penny eyes piercing through me, I feel sexy.

And it feels strange and awkward and beautiful all at the same time.

"I got something that I want to show you." Danny pops off the stool and motions for me to follow with his hand. I don't have to ask him where we're going. I know we're going to his bedroom.

"I borrowed it today from Mike Spitzer. He's one of the guys on the team."

I hover in his doorway, afraid to enter. My leg is brushing against his perfectly made bed with the pillow neatly tucked underneath his plaid Tommy Hilfiger comforter. I feel a lump forming in my throat, and I'm not even sure if I can speak. I want to sit on that bed with Danny. I want him to kiss me. In the corner, with his back to me, Danny is fidgeting with something. When he turns to face me, he holds out an acoustic guitar. "See," he says simply, as if I should know what he means.

"How did you know I play?" I ask, surprised.

"Marisol told me. I talked to her last night at homecoming." He smiles and pushes the guitar forward. "I thought maybe you would play something for me."

Play for him. I don't know what to say to that. Nobody had ever asked me to play for them—ever. "You and Marisol talked about me?" I ask quietly. He nods his head. "At homecoming?" I repeat. He nods his head again. "How was it? How was homecoming?" I ask. It's something I've wanted to ask him since I walked through the door.

"Okay, I guess." He presses the guitar into my hands. "If you're into that kind of thing. Would you?" he asks, pointing at the guitar.

In my hands, the guitar is cold and foreign and comforting. I strum it casually, trying to find the courage to give him what he really wants from me. "I really want to hear you play," he tells me, closer this time. He is just a fiber of carpet away.

"Do you like Marisol?" I say, stepping two fibers back. This question is urgently important to me. Anything to take us away from THIS.

"Marisol's cool." He pounds lightly on the wall with his fist.

"And?" I prompt him.

"And what?" The pounding increases. He looks over at me; his eyes burn holes through my heart. "She's nice. We talked last night at the dance when I was standing by the restroom waiting for . . . Tamara." He looks down, like he's aware that the mention of her name might ruin THIS.

"Sit." He drags me onto his bed, then scoots away from me as if I am on fire. He watches me expectantly. "Play," he instructs.

I rest the guitar on my knee and clear my mind, and then I pluck a whisper of a melody from some far-off place that I haven't quite seen. I hum it so that I can remember and let my fingers know what they are expected to play, and then, after I close my eyes and listen, I began to play with confidence. Before I know it I am singing, my voice husky, wobbly, and afraid. But still I am singing.

*I sang a lullaby as if to soothe your soul*
*And I sang it in a whisper to be heard by you alone*
*And in the moonlight of the night*
*I saw your lovely face*
*And I wondered if you'd comfort me . . .*
*Or if you'd let me stay.*

The words flow smoothly, like a sunny day in the back of my house, sitting between the palm trees that border my garden. In my mind, I picture Marisol there, feet propped over the edge of her bench, fingers curling in and out, eyes lost in the skies.

*I was lost inside your eyes*
*Lost inside your depth*
*Lost to everything but the sound of your own breath*
*And I wondered where you'd go*

*I wondered what you'd see
And I wondered if you'd realize the love inside of me.*

I play the chords. I know them well. Only a few weeks ago, I had cried while writing this song. I told myself I wasn't crying for anyone in particular, but for the beauty of the words, their longing. Now I wasn't so sure.

To the very end, I play with my eyes shut. When I finish, I lay the guitar in my lap and hum a little longer. My body is filled with electrical currents and bridges of uncertainty. I feel raw and exposed, like I handed Danny the keys to my diary and asked that he read it all out loud and understand.

Danny says something to quiet the silence. A heartbeat after the words leave his mouth, I have already forgotten them. I don't care about what he says, but how he says it. My whole body aches from his tone. I have mesmerized him.

I open my eyes, and frown at their wetness.

"That song," is all he says now.

"Yes," I say, "that song."

"That song," he repeats, as if I should know.

"Yes," I tell him. "That song." And then, when it is inevitable, "I know."

dinner is not what i feared. there is no fancy china pattern to contend with, Dalia (thankfully) does not wear her tiara, and Danny's father is not stuffy and he doesn't bore us to death by speaking about adult subject matters such as foreign policy and the Republicans' proposed tax cut for the upcoming year.

It's much better than that. There are plates that don't match and a chipped dining room table. There are his parents and Dalia. There is Danny and me. There is his cat, Max, and his grandfather who saves bread underneath the table to give to the ducks later that day. And I smile the whole way through, because dinner is nothing like what I expected and everything that I hoped it would be.

"What does your father do?" Mr. Diaz asks somewhere between the Cuban bread and the rice and beans.

"He's a literature professor at UM," I tell him.

"And your mother?"

"Um, she died in a car accident when I was nine."

"Oh," Mrs. Diaz says.

"Oh," Mr. Diaz says.

"I'm sorry, Susie. We didn't know," Mrs. Diaz apologizes. And Mr. Diaz shakes his head sympathetically, while Dalia looks away. Danny reaches for my hand underneath the table and then like a dream quickly takes it away.

"I didn't know," he says, looking at me, like I'm new to him, like in someway it all makes sense.

"I don't like to talk about it." I pick at my food. Shove broccoli around. Apparently, Dalia takes this as a signal to change the subject.

"Mami," she says, "are we or are we not going to Cuba this year?"

The conversation moves fast from there. Danny's parents tell me about their trips to Cuba and Spain and Portugal. I have seen the world, too, I tell his mom. My dad has a set of coffee table books that explore international travel. Danny laughs, and even Dalia smiles. It's all back to normal after that. And the best part is that I know I am a hit.

At the dinner table, I am a star.


after dinner, i follow mrs. diaz into the kitchen. i help her scrape leftover rice and black beans into containers. Then I offer to help her with dishes. "I don't mind," I assure her. "Really."

"Thanks." She smiles at me, the ends of her lips fluttering. "I don't know what it is, but I've always preferred to wash dishes by hand. My husband thinks I'm being stubborn, and you know what, maybe I am."

She fills the sink with soapy water and gives me a long look. "I wanted to thank you for coming over to dinner tonight. It really means a lot to us. We're really appreciative of you taking your time to help Danny pass this class."

"Thanks," I say softly. It was one of the nicest things an adult has ever said to me. "Thanks a lot." I dig my hands into the suds and feel the sting of the hot water. Mechanically, I begin to wash. I like washing dishes. It gives me time to think.

And right now, I'm thinking, why did I follow Mrs. Diaz into the kitchen instead of sitting just fifteen feet away in the family room with Danny?

Hmm . . . *Because if I went to the family room, I might eventually be left alone with Danny,* the voice in my head answers back—that is, after Dalia got tired of painting her toenails, and their grandfather finished reading *El Nuevo Herald,* and their father stopped snoozing in the La-Z-Boy recliner. But still, eventually it might have happened. And then what?

I still don't know why Danny invited me here. There are really only two logical reasons:

1. He likes me.

2. He likes Tamara, but still wants to thank me for being such a good tutor girl.

Nothing good can come from me obsessing about this now, so I sneak a glance at Mrs. Diaz. She's rinsing the dishes as I hand them to her, placing them in the dish rack next to her. We are totally in sync.

I like Mrs. Diaz. I like the way her voice curves when she speaks. And the way she seems to be aware of everyone else's needs. Like at dinner, she made sure everyone was served before she sat down. And there are the other little things. The way she rubs Danny's hand every time he makes her laugh. The way that Dalia, with her reputation as the wicked witch of OG, loosens up around her. The way that I can suddenly say what I think; admit the things that hurt me; confess to Danny that my mother is dead; and, afterward, hear those words ring in my ears without wanting to cry. Mrs. Diaz is like a great equalizer. Like, suddenly, the world is a little straighter when you're standing next to her.

"You know, my mother lost her mother at a very young age. I never even got to meet her," she tells me suddenly. Her voice is wistful. It surprises me. I drop a dish into the suds, sending bubbles splashing everywhere. Mrs. Diaz laughs. The sound gets stuck in her throat and tumbles out in small bits.

"I used to feel so sad for my mother when she'd pull out old photo albums and stare at her pictures." Mrs. Diaz shakes her head. Her eyes are distant, like she's back with her mother, back with those photo albums. "The love for a mother is phenomenal," she says, speaking for the both of us.

"I'm sorry." She wipes her hands with a dish towel. She turns to me. I look down, embarrassed. She rubs my shoulder with one dry hand. "I like you very much, Susie. You are an amazing girl. And, believe it or not, those are Danny's words, not mine." She takes a dish from my hand and dries it. "Which is why I want to share with you something about me, something personal."

I don't know what to say. Somehow I manage to lift my chin and look directly at her.

"About ten years ago when Danny and Dalia were only six, my mother died. I was heartbroken. The kids were heartbroken, too. We all lived together in Texas—one big, happy Cuban family unit. My father"—she points to her father, sitting next to Danny on the family room sofa—"was crushed. He could barely function. I had the hardest time getting him to eat. Basically, he wanted to die."

I look over at Danny's grandfather—Emmanuel is his name—and I try to picture him being so depressed. He doesn't seem to have the personality for it, not with the way he sits there silently chuckling to himself over the Sunday funnies.

"I know." Mrs. Diaz follows my eyes. "It's hard to believe now, but it's true."

"So what did you do?" Suddenly, it's super-important that I learn how Mrs. Diaz managed to resurrect her dad from the living dead. It's super-important because maybe I know someone whom I'd like to resurrect from the living dead.

"I didn't do anything. I mean, I tried." She makes the sign of the cross. "God knows I tried. But in the end, it took time."

"How much time?" I ask, my voice filled with disappointment.

She shakes her head sadly and places her hand next to mine on the countertop. "I'm afraid it took quite a bit of time."

"Oh." My body slumps a little, and I think about my dad, about how dating Leslie hasn't brought him back to life (not that I wanted him to come back to life for her, but still). How much more time can I give him? How much more time did we have before I stopped caring at all?

"Do you want to see something?" Mrs. Diaz walks out of the kitchen and returns a minute later with a photo album opened to a picture of a young bride and groom. "Isn't she beautiful?" I look at the photo and then back to Mrs. Diaz. They're nearly identical, except that Mrs. Diaz is like twenty years older than the woman in the picture was.

"Can I look?" I ask.

"Sure." Mrs. Diaz hands me the photo album and turns back to the half-tidied kitchen.

I lean against the countertop, Mrs. Diaz flittering around me, and start to flip through the pages. There are tons and tons of photos of friends, family, parties, and life. There is so much life in these pages. "Is this you?" I ask.

"Yeah." She turns toward me. "That was my *quince* party. You know, my sweet fifteen."

I turn the album back around and cradle it in my arms. The pages are worn, like someone has spent a lot of time reliving these memories. "Is this your album?" I ask.

"Yes," she says over her shoulder. "My mother made it for me a few years before she died. But"—her voice stretches thin as she reaches up to put a wineglass back in the cabinet—"my father keeps it in his room these days. He likes to remember."

"Oh." I flip the page to the very beginning and stop at an eight-by-ten black-and-white photo. It is a picture of Mrs. Diaz, about age ten. She is being held in her mother's arms. The girl smiles at the camera. Smiles at me. Pushes me to feeling things inside me, things that I haven't felt in so long.

"Are you okay?" Mrs. Diaz places her hand over mine. "You keep shaking your head."

There are so many things that I want to tell her. All these thoughts and feelings that have been sitting on the tip of my tongue for years. Words that I can't even say to Marisol, words that I can barely say to myself, but, for some reason, now, here with Mrs. Diaz, I want to say them all.

But once again, I can't. I'm just not ready.

"I'm fine." I thrust the photo album back at Mrs. Diaz. "I'm fine." But I'm not. I'm really not. In less than a week it will be the six-year anniversary of my mother's death and to me, it still feels like yesterday. What if there are some wounds that time can't heal? What if certain people—people like my father, people like me—can live a lifetime without ever being capable of letting go of the hurt? I hope it's not true, but what if it is? Is it always going to be like this for me?

She squeezes my hand. "You know, Susie, I just might understand," she says quietly.

"Oh." I shake my head, embarrassed. I use all my energy to make my eyes meet hers. "I'm fine . . . Is there a bathroom that I can use? I think I drank too much water."

"Sure." She smiles kindly at me, that same smile that Danny gave me in the yearbook line. Kind. Reassuring. Forgiving. "There's one down the hall."

"Thanks." I speed-walk to the bathroom, and even then with it being barely seven strides away, I make it just before the tears start to fall. I turn on the faucet, sit on the toilet, and listen to the water run and run. I ask myself all the questions that I've asked myself before. I ask myself all the questions that never change: Why can't I let this go? Why can't I move on?

And then I give myself the only answer that I know:

Because she loved me. And I loved her. She loved me, and I'll never be the same.

# TWENTY-FOUR

# falling

* * *

"what happened to you?" the next day at school danny
finds me in the library, deep in the reference section.

"What do you mean?" I don't really look him in the eyes. I'm still
too embarrassed.

"My mom said that one minute you guys were talking and the next
minute you were gone." He turns me so that we are facing each other
in the aisle. "Hey," he says, lifting my chin up. "I'm talking to you."

"That's all she said?" My voice quivers a bit because his hand is
still on my chin.

"Yeah." His hand drops to his side, and he kind of takes a step
back. "Yeah," he repeats, his voice a little husky.

He takes a deep breath. "Are you, um, okay?"

"Yeah, I'm fine," I tell him, but I know that I'm not. Everything is
slipping, slipping away. I turn back to the reference books and busy
myself looking for something, although I don't remember what.
Maybe if I just busy myself enough, he'll leave me alone and go back
to his friends. I don't know why he talks to me so much lately or why
when no one is looking, he finds all these little ways to touch me. I

don't understand anything about Danny except sometimes when he looks at me, it's like he really sees me. ME. Why that matters, I don't know. But it does.

He unzips his book bag and takes something out. Then, like it's the most natural thing in the world, our hanging out with no previous plans, no specified reason—he slumps down onto the floor, sits Indian style, and starts reading something. I look over my shoulder to see what it is. He's reading *The Picture of Dorian Gray*. It's the next book on his list. He must be getting a head start.

I study his face while he's reading—his thick, black lashes and mocha skin. I think about the conversation we had after I played the guitar at his house on Sunday. I had made fun of him for owning so many *Star Wars* action figures.

"But they're classics. There's a difference," he told me.

I asked him who he would rather be, Han Solo or Luke Sky-walker?

"Han Solo," he said.

"Why?" We were sitting on his bed, close enough that I could smell his Zest. "'Cause he gets the girl," he replied, hitting me softly with a raggedy teddy bear.

"But Princess Leia wasn't that pretty," I told him, grabbing the bear, pulling it out of his reach.

"She was to him," he said, snatching the bear out of my hands and hitting me on the head with a furry leg.

"Is that all that matters?" I asked, reaching for the bear, but ending up with my hands grabbed and pulled over my head.

"What?" he said as we struggled. His face was inches from mine and I could smell the faintest bit of mint. His teeth were really, really white.

"Let me go, I can't breathe." We were too close. I might have twitched.

"Okay, but first"—he pulled my hands behind my back so that our chests were pressed against each other and I could feel his heart beating—"I have to tell you something."

"What?" I whispered. My voice caught in my throat.

"That," Danny whispered back, "you are pretty to me."

"You're acting strange." Danny's real voice cuts through my memory. I realize he was pretending to read his book.

"No." I grab a reference book and slide down onto the carpet next to him. "I'm not." But I am. I wonder if I should tell him about my mom's memorial service this weekend. I wonder if I should share that with him.

"Yes, you are." Danny's eyes fall down to my lap. He reaches across the space between us and tilts the reference book up so he can read its title. "*The History of Automotive Mechanics*?" he says, trying not to laugh. "Strange."

I look at the spine of the book. Sure enough, it is *The History of Automotive Mechanics*. Then I flip it over so he can't see the title. Not that it matters anymore.

"I just wanted to look at something in here." I clear my throat. "That's all."

"Yeah." He reaches back for the book. "Let me see."

"No." I hold on tightly. "Leave it alone."

"Fine." His hand falls away from the book and rests on my thigh.

"Um." I look down at his hand, waiting for him to move it. But he just leaves it there, like it's the most usual thing in the world for him to have his hand resting on my thigh.

It's so intimate, what he's doing. So casual. It warms me up. I've never even held hands with a boy before, and I wonder how it would feel to have Danny's hand wrap over mine. Would it create the same burning sensation that I am feeling now? Like my thigh is being eaten alive by acid. Would my hand get lost inside of his? His hands are large. The veins protrude like thick green highways that disappear beneath the neat edges of his Abercrombie & Fitch T-shirt.

"Susie?" Danny stops short, and I think that it feels so good to hear him say my name. I wish he would say my name over and over and over again.

"What?" I feel a tingle in my belly that stretches down to the soft space between my thighs.

"Susie, sit closer to me." His voice fades away, like clouds that disappear after a summer rain.

"Why?" I whisper.

"Because," he says, like that's reason enough.

"No," I answer back, because a *because* is definitely not reason enough to do what he is asking me to do.

"Susie—"

"Stop saying my name. I'm right here." *But please don't ever stop saying my name.*

"Susie." Not my name followed by a question mark. But my name, period. "Fine."

He picks up his book, pretends to read again. I read *The History of Automotive Mechanics.* I flip open to the middle of the book and start to learn about the sixties.

"Are you really reading?" he asks a few minutes later.

"Yes." I peer at him over my three-hundred-plus-page book, which I noted several seconds earlier is the first volume in a three-volume series. "You?"

"No," he says, "I'm not."

"Well," I keep my voice light, even though my heart is *thump-thump-thump*ing away, "what are you doing?"

"I'm watching you read."

"Oh." Oh.

"Susie . . ." He scurries closer to me. His jeans make a rubbing noise along the carpet, and then his face is next to mine. He is tracing my face with his breath, inhaling my scent with his lips. "Susie," he says, because, apparently, saying my name is enough to tell me everything he's trying to tell me. And maybe it is. Maybe.

"Danny."

And then, in the library, our bodies as close as possible, we kiss. Very, very, slowly.

### "you kissed him!"

Curled up under the covers of Marisol's bed, I describe every single taste I felt as Danny's tongue entered my mouth.

"It was sweet, like corn."

"I bet you it was," Marisol says. "I saw someone eating corn in the cafeteria today." Marisol sits upside down with her legs on the bed, her back on the floor, and her butt somewhere in between.

"So? What did he say afterward? And why didn't the librarian catch you? She would have sent you to the office."

"I don't know. He didn't really say much and then Dalia showed up suddenly and took him away. They had to finish a science project they were working on."

"Did Dalia catching you kissing?" Marisol asks.

"Yeah, kind of. And then he said, 'I'll see you tomorrow at lunch.'" Like I have enough patience to wait for lunch tomorrow?

"Tomorrow at lunch? He wants to eat lunch with you. Well, that's huge."

"I know," I squeal, burying my head in her pillows. "I know."

"The only problem is that we eat lunch at the canal. We don't eat at school." Marisol shrugs like she's saying *oh well*. I think she's still a bit bitter about giving up her new lunch routine (eating with Ryan in the cafeteria) to rejoin me in our old lunch routine (eating together at the canal).

"Well, he can come, too." I don't care if Marisol is inconvenienced. I remember homecoming. I look at her and she remembers it, too.

"Fine." Marisol gives me a look. "He can come, too. But on Wednesday, you are either eating lunch with me and Ryan in the cafeteria or you're eating by yourself."

"Fine," I tell her. And for the first time in a long time, I am happy.

TWENTY-FIVE

# relationships

• • •

walking to the canal the next day, danny and i are very, very awkward. Thankfully, Marisol does all the talking.

"It's going to rain big-time," she says, pointing at the dark clouds. "There better not be any lightning." She looks at Danny. "I'm petrified of lightning."

"Yeah?" Danny says. "Well, isn't Florida like the lightning capital of the world?"

"It is," I say, which is pretty much my entire contribution to the conversation.

Then Marisol talks about her first-period class (chemistry) and moves all the way to sixth period (algebra II), and Danny and I listen and listen and listen.

"Do you know Ms. Morris?" Marisol asks Danny. She walks between us, trying to connect the distance that has left us one hundred miles apart in a two-second radius. "She's crazy. She made us do fifty math problems in class yesterday without being able to resharpen our pencils. She says the noise irritates her and that our parents can afford mechanical pencils. Then she got mad when the entire class only made it to problem twenty-two before their pencils were dull. You should have seen her face. . . ."

She waits for us to laugh, but we don't. "It was really funny." Marisol plops down on the grass and unwraps her sub. "I guess you had to be there."

Danny and I stare down at Marisol. I'm waiting for Danny to sit before I sit. And Danny is waiting for something. What it is, I don't know.

"You know," Danny says, listening to the thunder rolling across the canal, "I live right over there."

"Which one is it?" Marisol asks, looking nervously at the sky.

"The one with the three mango trees." He points five houses over. "Right there."

"Do you have a microwave?" Marisol asks, when lightning cracks overhead. She holds up her chicken parmesan, nervously. "This is cold."

"I do," Danny answers rather redundantly.

"Let's go."


we make it to danny's house before the rain hits.

"Wow," Marisol says ducking in through the sliding glass door. "That's going to be bad."

The three of us stand in the doorway, watching the rain pour down. Lightning zigzags across the sky.

"Maybe we shouldn't use electrical appliances." Marisol stares at her sub. I can tell she's wondering whether the sandwich is worth being electrocuted.

"Here." Danny takes it from her, tosses it in the microwave, and turns back to me. When the microwave dings, he hands the sub back to Marisol and she takes it to the family sofa, where she's already started reading the first of ten *Us* magazines stacked on the coffee table.

"Marisol's addicted to *Us*," I tell Danny.

"So is Dalia. She's got a subscription."

Danny and I eat at the bar. He sips noisily from his glass of water, but I don't mind. I like knowing that in some way he is flawed, even if it's a little flaw.

"That really does look bad." Danny nods his head toward the sliding glass door. Outside the rain is falling sideways, with lightning cracking every five minutes.

Danny looks at the clock on the microwave. We have thirty minutes left for lunch. "I don't know if that's going to stop," he says.

"Maybe we should check the Weather Channel," I suggest.

"I vote for the Weather Channel," Marisol screeches from the sofa, visibly rising when the next bolt hits. "Definitely Weather Channel."

We settle in front of the TV. Marisol moves as deep into the sofa cushions as humanly possible.

"Oh, tornado watch," Marisol announces over the announcer. "That's not good."

"No, not in this county," Danny says, trumping Marisol. "Palm Beach and Broward," he reads.

"But hello?" Marisol's voice is filled with dread. "Lightning. Do you want to walk in that?"

"We could try. We have twenty minutes to make it," I point out. And then the television goes black.

"Electricity went out," Danny observes.

"Where is your grandpa?" I ask. "Maybe he can drive us?"

"Aunt Ana's day." Danny ruffles his hair with his fingers. "We should stay," he decides. "That's bad. Hope nobody has a test or anything."

"Nope," Marisol says, wrapping a knitted blanket from the corner of the couch around her, and pulling her *Us* magazines closer. "I'm good."

"You?" Danny asks me.

"Nope," I say. "But won't we get in trouble?" I've never actually skipped before. What if my dad finds out?

"Maybe," Marisol says, "but look at that."

"Yeah," I say, looking at the rain falling sideways, and the water on the canal growing a little choppy, "look at that." I guess some things are just out of my control.

# TWENTY-SIX

# moments

. . .

"how long?" danny watches me through hooded eyes. he says the rain always makes him tired.

The carpet in Danny's bedroom is soft. We are lying side by side, not touching, yet sharing each other's space. In the family room, Marisol reads on, oblivious to all that I have learned about Danny.

"Three weeks, but it sucked. I had to stick a pencil in it because it itched so much. And then, one time, I had Marisol scratch underneath it with a short ruler, and we lost it. It just slid right to the middle and we couldn't get it out."

Danny laughs, and I smile because he thinks I'm funny.

"Look. There you go again, proving you can smile."

"Shut up." I turn on my side to face him. "I told you I can smile."

"Yeah." Danny smiles back at me. "I remember that." He turns on his side. "Okay, check this out. One time I broke my ankle, and I had to wear a cast, and Dalia thought it would be funny to shove M&M's down it while I was sleeping. When I woke up I thought something was in there but I didn't know what. I just felt like there were all these small balls in my cast. So," Danny laughs, "I went outside to get my mom and she was talking to my grandfather. By the time she got to look at my ankle, the M&M's had melted and there was chocolate oozing onto my toes."

"You and Dalia really like each other, don't you?" I ask.

"Yeah, we're twins, so that goes a long way."

"I wish I had a twin," I tell him.

"You do." He smiles sleepily. "Marisol."

We stop talking for a while, lie back, and listen to the rain. I think of a list of questions that I would like to ask Danny:

1. Where were you born?

2. How old were you when you lost your first tooth?

3. Who was your first kiss?

4. Why did you invite Tamara to homecoming instead of me?

5. Do you want me to be your girlfriend?

6. Why did you kiss me in the library?

7. Could you tell that you were my first kiss?

8. Do you really think I am pretty?

9. Why won't you hold my hand?

Beside me, Danny seems less bothered by the unknown and more willing to meditate to the hypnotic pulse of the thunderstorm. He breathes deeply and then, without warning, there is a twitch. A quick movement of his hand followed by a lifting of shoulders. I roll on my side to watch him. He is sleeping, mouth open, drooling. His hand a second away from mine.

I decide to take the plunge.

I scoot toward him until I can scoot no more, and then, very quietly, I roll myself into his arms.

an hour later, i roll over on my side and collide with a solid object. I open my eyes and find myself nose to nose with Danny.

"Hey," he says casually.

"Mm-hmm," I mutter.

"You fell asleep. It's two thirty." His breath curls around my face, and I want to nuzzle farther into him. I've never been this close to anyone in my life.

"Mm-hmm," I mutter. My eyes fall shut and I'm dangerously close to falling back to sleep.

"You have to go." He nudges me. "School's out. And my mom gets off work early today."

"Oh crap." I stand.

"Slow down," Danny says. "You've got fifteen minutes."

"But what if your mom finds us here?" I run around the room, looking for evidence that I've been here.

"What are you looking for?" Danny asks lazily from the floor.

"Evidence." Pieces of me, I think. "Where are my socks?" I ask perplexed.

"On your feet." He smiles up at me as if I'm insane.

"Oh." I stare down at my socks. I wonder if they've just returned from the witness protection program.

"Where's Marisol?"

"In the bathroom," he says. "I just saw her walk in there like two minutes ago."

"Oh, okay." I step over Danny and race toward the sound of water splashing.

"Hey—" Danny moans from the floor. His hand snakes out and grabs hold of my ankle. "Wait," he pleads.

"But I have to leave before your mom gets home."

"I know," he says gently. "But this will only take a second."

"What?" I shake my ankle from his reach.

"I like you," he says quickly. I stop in my tracks.

"I—" My words falter before they leave the starting gate. I try again, but I can't think clearly. Words are not part of this.

"She likes you, too," Marisol says from the doorway. And then with a wicked smile, she grabs my hand and drags me to safety.

# TWENTY-SEVEN

# elation

. . .

"i have something to tell you," marisol says. we're sitting on
my bed, wrapped in separate comforters, half talking, half lying
around and being lazy.

"What?" My voice is muffled by the pillow. I'm still a bit sleepy.

"Well, when I had that talk with Danny during homecoming
while Tamara was in the bathroom," she says, "I might have given
him the impression that you liked him."

"Marisol . . ." My voice is calm, but I'm not. At least not inside.
"Tell me exactly what you said."

"Nothing." She lifts the comforter over her face so that one eye
peeks out. "I just thought that it was so obvious that you two liked
each other and well . . . I wanted to move things along for you. Are
you mad?" she asks hesitantly.

"Mad," I huff. "Mad," I repeat more deflated. Why should I be?
Danny liked me. I couldn't have asked for better results.

"Just tell me everything you told him."

"Okay." The blanket slides off her face and she shimmies up, so
that she's sitting straight. She pulls her wet hair into a bun and uses a

rubber band from my nightstand table to secure it. She clears her throat. "Okay, first I asked him whether Tamara had asked him to homecoming or if he had asked her."

Is it possible that he didn't even ask her?

"Well, he *had* asked her." Marisol touches my hand, her way of softening the blow. "But he also said it was a direct result of you"—Marisol points her finger at me accusingly—"telling him that Tamara liked him. Otherwise, he would have never thought of inviting her. And then he said that he really wanted to invite someone else."

"Someone else? Who?"

"He didn't say, and I didn't ask. I just wanted him to talk—and, by the way, can I say thank God that Tamara was taking her good old sweet time in the bathroom, and Ryan had trouble getting the zipper on his rented tux back up, because if not, the conversation would have been super-brief, but"—Marisol takes a huge gulp of air as if she's about to let out a major secret—"he did say that the person he wanted to ask said that she didn't really want to be asked, anyway."

"You think he was talking about me?" I ask nervously.

"What other girl in America would tell someone as hot as Danny that they didn't want to go to homecoming?" Marisol raises both of her eyebrows accusingly.

"But then why invite Tamara at all?" I think about him slow dancing with Tamara and my heart skips a beat. Then I think about rolling myself into Danny's arms. The two images collide, and suddenly I feel nauseated.

"I don't know. I didn't ask. But didn't you say that Mrs. Diaz said Dalia bought the tickets way in advance? Maybe he already had the extra ticket? It's possible." Marisol shrugs her shoulders.

"Wow. Oh, wow. You think?" I ask. How cool would that be if it were true? That would mean that Tamara was his date by DEFAULT!

"Maybe," Marisol says. "You never know."

"Okay, so get to the part where you tell Danny that I like him."

"Give me some credit." Marisol gives me a dirty look. "I didn't exactly say, 'Oh, and by the way did you know that my best friend likes you?' I just said that I wished Susie were here, but she's so shy about guys that anyone who probably wanted to ask her would have thought that she didn't want to be asked, but that that wasn't necessarily the case. And then I thanked him for the Beatles CD and that was it." Done with her story, Marisol snuggles back into the covers.

"That's it?" I lean my head against the wall. That wasn't nearly enough! I wanted more, and more, and more. I wanted it all.

"So," Marisol mutters sleepily, "what do you think?"

"I think," I tell Marisol, "that you did good."

"I know." She sighs. "I always do."

# TWENTY-EIGHT

# thanksgiving

. . .

even with danny in my life, the next few days pass in a blur. The closer I get to my mother's memorial service, the harder it is for me to feel . . . normal.

When Thanksgiving arrives a few days later, it's just me and my dad. All the other usual suspects have disappeared:

1. Grandma and Grandpa are in Boston with Aunt Emily, although I bet Grandma still thinks she's here in Miami.

2. Marisol is somewhere on South Beach, probably trying to hold down her meal. It's going to be a tough fight, since she's spending Thanksgiving with her Dad and his life-sized Barbie, a.k.a. his new, annoying girlfriend.

3. Leslie's in the Bahamas on a three-day minivacation with several of her coworkers. I imagine they're painting their toenails peaceful pastels while psychoanalyzing the crap out of each other.

And then there's me and my dad. Alone.

We make the most of the day. We sit in front of the TV and watch the Macy's parade. We don't talk a lot, but that's not unusual. Still, somehow, words work their way out.

"That's interesting," I say at one point.

"Yeah," he says, some time later.

"Can you believe they used that tired theme again?" I ask.

"Can you turn up the volume?" he asks. "I'd like to hear what he's saying."

Then we eat a simple meal: two TV dinners, two Capri Suns. Nothing fancy in our house.

When the sun goes down, we go our separate ways. Like always.

# TWENTY-NINE

# saturday

• • •

on saturday, november twenty-sixth, i remember the death of my mother. Alone. My father is off on his own. I don't know where he goes. I've never asked. I don't want to know.

I have my own rituals, my own way of dealing with things. And maybe it's best that we don't share this day. Maybe it's best that it stays this way.

So I wake up, I sit in my garden, and I talk to myself. I say, "Today is the day that my mother died." I don't say it to be melodramatic. I say it to make it real. Because sometimes it feels like I'll never fully understand. Like my mind isn't big enough to comprehend that I will never see her again.

Then I remember, because that's what today is for. I remember how when I was small and scared, I used to crawl underneath her shirt and wrap my arms super-tight around her waist. She tried to get me to let her go, but I wouldn't. I couldn't.

I remember the way she laughed when I made my fish face. And that she had her right ear double pierced, and she promised that I could get mine double pierced, too, on my twelfth birthday.

I remember that she liked to read Danielle Steel books before going to bed at night. And that she would lay my head on her lap and clean the inside of my ears with a wet Q-tip. I remember so much about her.

And then I wonder why I remember so much about her and so very little about my dad. My specific memories of him start on the day she died.

Him, at the hospital, talking to the doctors. Me, trying to read his lips, trying to see what they were saying. Him, standing tall, then suddenly his shoulders drooping like somebody sucked the life out of him. The doctor walking away from him, shaking his head, cleaning his glasses with the hem of his pristine white jacket. My dad, there, on the floor, leaning his head against the wall. The hours that passed and passed and passed until I called Grandma and Grandpa and they came to take us home.

Him, next to her coffin, holding her cold hand for so long I thought he'd get frostbite. Me, next to him, watching the way his legs trembled.

I remember it all because I have to remember. I have to let her know that I remember. Because today is the day that my mother died. Saturday. November twenty-sixth.

# THIRTY

# sunday, the memorial

●  ●  ●

on sunday my grandfather brings my grandmother over early and leaves with my father to get ready for the big day.

Because my grandmother has trouble remembering lately, I'm supposed to keep an eye on her. So I sit with her in the living room, partially watching her, partially trying to distract myself by reading a book. She's watching me, too.

Although my grandmother's crazy, she's not really crazy. She's in the early stages of Alzheimer's, which is just a fancy way of saying that 50 percent of the time she has absolutely no clue who I am. Which sucks. I guess.

Today is pretty much no different. She's on her end of the sofa chitchattering about this and that, talking about all kinds of dead people, when suddenly she looks at me and says: "You look a lot like your mother."

That's it. "You look a lot like your mother." And then she's gone. Moseying her way back to senility. Leaving me to wonder exactly what she means.

"your uncle martin rubbed up on me." later, over the fruit platter, Marisol and I gossip. "I think he's finally reached the age where he's senile."

"I think he was senile when he hit ninety. Now he's pretty much infantile." We both turn to Uncle Martin sitting on the sofa in the living room, drool running down his chin.

"I want to go before I'm eighty-five," Marisol says. "That way I'll at least have some decency."

"Don't worry," I assure her. "If you make it to eighty-five, I'll throw you off a bridge." I start to smile but then fall short.

"Don't you find it weird that Marc is here?" Marisol nods in Marc's direction. He's sitting with his parents at the dining room table.

"No." I take a long sip of my tea, which I'm drinking because it's supposed to calm my nerves. "It's different now, I think." I'm pretty sure that once a guy has cried on your shoulder, it will be different for the rest of your life.

"Well, what about Tamara? I can't believe she had the nerve to show up here with her parents." We turn to look at Tamara, decked out in her it's-Sunday-and-I'm-at-a-memorial-service best. "She's such a bitch," Marisol snaps. "I bet you she came just because she's hoping to run into Danny. She knows you two are together now."

"How do you know that? It's only been a few days of whatever."

"I don't know how," Marisol says, "but she does. Abby, her best friend, asked me what was going on between you two. She said you stole Danny away from her."

"I what?" I want to laugh. If I weren't at my mother's memorial service, I would. "Are you kidding?"

"Nope." Marisol shakes her head and raises her hand, like she's being sworn into office or something. "God's honest truth."

"Whatever." Crap like this seems so petty to me today.

"I guess. So, where's Danny?" Marisol looks around, as if between the two adjoining twelve-by-thirteen rooms, she might have possibly missed him. Then she checks her watch. "He's coming, right?"

"No."

"Why not?" She picks at the fruit on the table. "He does know, right?"

"Nope." I turn my head away, hoping that my subtle body language will communicate that this is not a conversation I want to have with her. But of course it doesn't.

"Why didn't you invite him?"

I shrug. "Didn't feel like it."

"But he knows about your mother, right?" she asks, looking over at the front door.

"Yeah, I told him. But *this* is different." I look over at Uncle Martin. He is leaning kind of crooked against the sofa. His daughter, Cecile, is trying to straighten him by shoving a pillow behind his back, but it isn't working. "If I'm not dead by ninety, throw me off a bridge."

"Sure," Marisol says. Then a few seconds later, she mutters, "Maybe I'll throw you a little earlier."

"What's that supposed to mean?" I give her a look.

"Just wondering why you're avoiding my questions."

"I'm not."

We turn back to the fruit platter. The fruit platter is safe. It's freaking Switzerland. It's not I'd-like-to-kill-my-best-friend territory. Marisol picks up a grape and studies it intently. "I invited Ryan."

"What?" My mouth falls open in disbelief. "I thought he was going skiing this weekend with his family."

"Nope, he got out of it. He didn't want to go without me," she adds rather smugly.

"Why would you do that? Why would you invite him *here?*"

"I don't know," she says, suddenly realizing that she's miscalculated the level of pissed-off I would be. "I just did." Her voice shrinks, and she looks away. "I didn't think it would be such a big deal. I thought you'd invite Danny." She touches my shoulder. "Hey, don't be mad."

"You should have talked to me!" I was so angry at her that I could feel my insides shaking. This was my loss. *My* loss. Did she think my mother's memorial service was, like, a house party?

"I tried calling you last night, but you wouldn't answer your phone. You wouldn't talk to me—"

"It was the anniversary of my mother's death—"

"I know," she cuts me off, "but you still could have talked to me. So I called Ryan. I was upset because I knew that you were shutting me out, and I told him. And he said he'd come. You know," she says weakly, "for moral support."

"You shouldn't have invited him. This is private. For me, this is private."

"Susie." Marisol sets the grape down and grabs my arms so that I'm forced to turn to her. "I understand how hard this is for you. But you've got to start letting it go. It's not a private thing. It's something that happened to you. And your father. And your grandparents. And me. And my mom. You know, they were good friends. It's something that happened to all of us. Not just you. Besides, Tamara and Marc are here, too."

I look over at Tamara talking away to her mother, and Marc sitting uncomfortably between his parents, trying to loosen his black tie. And then I look at Leslie, rubbing my father's arm consolingly. The doorbell rings. Marisol takes a step forward and then looks at me. "It's probably Ryan," she says apologetically.

"I'm going to the garden." I set my teacup on the table and put my hand on my stomach. It hurts terribly, like someone is kneading my flesh into meatballs.

"Susie," Marisol's voice wavers. "This is hard for me, too, sometimes."

"Yeah," I look over at Marisol's mother still rubbing MY father's arm. "I can see that."

"Susie," Marisol begins, but the doorbell cuts her off.

"Answer it," I tell her, knowing that she will. And, when she walks away, hating myself for being right.

Alone now, I look back at my dad, trying hard to concentrate on what our neighbor, Mr. Mickles, is saying. Then I look at Leslie. She's nodding in agreement, standing so close to my father that the corner of her silk blouse is touching the left arm of his cotton jacket. I guess she's lending him her form of "moral support." Then I look at Marisol, standing in the doorway, smiling up at Ryan, his hand protectively holding hers.

And I try to figure out how, somewhere along the line, everything changed. For a long time, the three of them—my dad, Marisol, and Leslie—were all that I had. And that worked for me. For all of us. But not anymore. I know that because here we are, all three of us together. And I still feel so very alone.

# THIRTY-ONE

# fragmented sunday afternoon

．．．

somehow i find my way outside. amazingly, nobody is sitting in the garden. Today has turned out to be one of those freak days at the end of November that makes you think it's still summer. But the heat doesn't bother me. I sit on my bench and wait. And after a while, I try to be one of those girls who sits on a bench in her garden and cries for, like, dramatic purposes. But the tears won't come, just an ache that begins in my abdomen and spreads to my chest, and starts to really, really hurt.

I try to control the pain. I count my breaths. I flex my hands in and out. I bite my lip. Nothing works. I'm stuck in a perpetual state of panic.

later that day, i wander into my parents' bedroom. or i should say my parents' old bedroom. My dad doesn't come in here much. His clothes, his work, his entire life has somehow moved into the study, and when he needs to *sleep* (which in Dad language means rest his eyes for all of five seconds), he lies horizontally on the sofa in the study.

In my parents' old bedroom everything is pretty much the same. Except now when the door creaks open, I smell dust instead of my mom's Estée Lauder perfume.

One day, I made the mistake of asking my dad why we just didn't sell the house. Just up and move. I guess what I was saying was, *Why don't we move on?* Anyway, the look that he gave me was so strange, like someone had stitched invisible strings into his face and then pulled those strings downward as fast as they could. His eyes, his cheeks, his mouth, everything dropped into one big puddle of grief. It doesn't make sense to describe. It's one of those things that has to be seen for itself. I know. But still. That look. I'll never forget it.

after my mother died, i saw my father less and less. he woke me up in the morning and later said good night, but what happened between those two markers of the day, I can't say. I mean, I knew that he was in his study or at work, but other than that, I have no clue.

Maybe I'm partially to blame for the distance. It's not like I ever tell my father how lonely I feel, even when he's around. Particularly when he *is* around. I don't tell him how the door to his room seems to make room only for those who exit and never for those who wish to enter.

One time when I was eleven, I stood outside his study with my nose pushed against the pressed-wood door. My bare feet stuck underneath the crack. I wanted to see what would happen. I wanted to see how long it would take him to notice. It was a Saturday, I believe.

I stood there all day. I measured time by my heartbeat. First seconds passed. Then minutes. Then hours. And I thought about my father, about who he was, and how I no longer knew what to say to him. In the vacuum of my mother's death, I had been abandoned.

in my parents' room, i lie on my mother's side of the bed. I listen to the voices outside. I watch the light fade through the partially cracked vertical blinds. I count time. I try to be the type of girl who cries herself to sleep on her dead mother's bed. But this time, I really try only for dramatic purposes.

I do eventually fall asleep, wrapped in my mother's robe, my head resting on her pillow.

Some time later, I wake up. Marc is sitting next to me. His legs hang over the side of the bed. His back rests against the headboard. He's watching me.

"What are you doing *in here*?" My voice is rough like sandpaper.

"What else?" He holds out a half-empty bottle of wine. "Drinking."

I sit up. My head is pounding. And my stomach hurts even worse now. My heart is *rat-tat-tat*ting along my rib cage.

*"Why are you here?"* I wipe the sleep from my eyes, remembering that day when Danny wiped the drool from my cheek.

"I don't know. I saw you come in here, and I waited for you to come out, but you never did. So I came in. Can you believe they're still going out there?" He tilts his head and listens to the din of conversation coming from outside the room.

"What time is it?" I ask. My throat is itchy from dust and dry from sleep.

"I don't know." He takes a slow sip of the wine and hands it to me. I take a small sip to keep the cobwebs from my throat. It tastes sweet. A rush of heat fills my abdomen and spreads over my chest and lips.

"Let's get drunk," he says a minute later.

"Huh?" I turn to look at him. What is he thinking?

"Let's get drunk," he repeats and hands me the bottle. "Why the fuck not? I don't want to be here," he says. "You don't want to be here." He hands me the bottle and I take it, not really sure what I'm doing or what I'm thinking. Or if I'm thinking at all. "So, let's get drunk and then it'll be like we're not even here at all."

"But what if someone walks in? What if someone catches us?" It seems like an obvious concern. Though the fact that I'm asking questions makes me realize that I'm considering the possibility of getting drunk with Marc. Which I am. I TOTALLY AM.

I mean, what do I have to lose? I don't want to be here—not with Leslie rubbing my father's arm; not with Marisol, who's probably making out in the backyard with Ryan; and not with my crazy grandmother who doesn't even know who I am.

And with Marc? Do I want to be here with Marc? Why aren't I here with Danny?

"Well?" He nudges the bottle. Slowly, I lift it to my lips and take a long sip. I hand the bottle back to Marc and hiccup self-consciously.

"Slow down." Marc takes his turn. He puts the bottle to my lips, gives me a short sip.

"Where's Marisol?" I ask.

"Last time I saw her, she was outside in the garden with Ryan."

"Oh." It figures. Any doubts I have suddenly wash away.

"More?" he asks.

"Sure. Why not?"

when it's all gone, marc contemplates sneaking another bottle out of the living room.

"What do you think?" he asks.

"No." I lean my head against the headboard and watch the room spin around. Except for holidays, I don't drink. And even then, it's normally a few sips of wine from my grandfather's wineglass.

"How do you feel?" Marc asks, giving me a sloppy shove so that he can fit his entire body on the bed.

"Half retarded," I reply, and we laugh. "What times is it?"

"You already asked me that. I don't know."

"Well, find out." I shove him hard so that he almost falls over the bed.

"Hey." Marc pushes me back. Then he leans across me so that his chest is pressed against my thighs.

"What are you doing?" I look down at his body in my lap. It makes me laugh.

"Telling you the time." He reaches for an object on the night-stand table. "Seven p.m., I think."

Slowly, Marc pulls himself off me. His face is near me. It swims in my eyes. "Are you okay?" he asks.

"Are you?" Why were there two of him?

"Yeah. Are you?" He rubs the hair from my eyes. He leans down and I can smell his breath just inches from my nostrils. It smells like potato salad and wine.

"You know what . . ." he says, his face too close. "You look a lot like your mother." Absently he traces the area around my eyes and lets his fingers rest on my temple.

"Everyone keeps telling me that," I whisper because he's too close to speak in a normal tone.

He stares at me.

"You seem different tonight," I say, to stop him from staring at me.

"That's because I'm not an idiot tonight." He moves away from me, closes his eyes. I follow his lead. They feel so much better shut.

"You never answered my question," he says sleepily. He lays his head on my shoulder, and I can feel his heartbeat on my arm.

"What are you doing?" I open my eyes. This is all so weird.

"Nothing," he yawns. "Question: does it bother you that you look like your mother? Don't think," he tells me when I hesitate, "just say the first thing that comes into your mind."

"No, not if I really looked like her," I tell him.

He rolls over on his back and tucks his arms underneath his head.

"Do you remember that night that your mom was babysitting me, and I cut my hand with the kitchen knife?" His voice cuts in and out. At least to me it does. "Do you remember?"

"Yeah." I picture Marc in my kitchen, bawling his eyes out. He looks so little in my mind. It's hard to think about him as being little. But he was, at one point. And so was I.

"Oh my God, I cried for like an hour. I was such a pussy." He laughs, shakes the bed with it. "And your mom was so nice. She wrapped my hand in a towel and found that butterfly bandage that she had, and cleaned out my cut and then held me in her lap for like two hours. Do you remember?" Marc turns on his side and our eyes meet.

"Yeah," I tell him. "I remember."

"And she put us in bed, and made us something stupid like hot chocolate. And you were scared because there was all this blood and so she sat between us in your bed and put one arm around each of us and read to us that story that you liked so much. What story was that?"

"*The Giving Tree*," I tell him, though I can barely find my voice. It's hiding behind a wall of tears that is building in my throat.

"My mom never did shit like that. She was too busy. Busy with my father. Busy with her business. Busy with the dog. I don't even know if she likes me."

"I'm sure she likes you," I whisper. What else can I say?

"Maybe . . . Whatever . . . But that day I remember, like, all the time. I don't know why. It's like I love your mom for that stupid day." His voice is weak. "Is that possible?"

I try to speak, but it's hard. The tears make it too hard for me to tell him that I do think it's possible to have lifelong feelings from one single moment.

"Hey—" His hand brushes across my cheek. "Hey, now." His breathing is moist. "You do look like your mom. It freaks me out." He stares at me, through me, into me. He presses himself against me, and the tears come quickly now.

He brushes his lips over mine.

"No," I say quietly. "Don't." But he doesn't listen. He lays himself on top of me. His body covers mine from head to toe. He takes my arms and wraps them around his waist. "Please," he whispers. His tongue pushes my mouth open, gets lost in its warmth. His tongue is soft, reassuring, kind.

"You taste sweet," he murmurs. His lips graze my eyes, my ears, the tip of my nose, and then a path down my neck. "Sweet, like a cough drop."

His hands rub hesitantly along my sides. I close my eyes. My thoughts swirl hazily.

I think about Danny. I think about our kiss in the library. I think about Halloween, his body between my thighs, my hand in his hair. I think about Danny and slowly I find myself kissing Marc back.

It may be seconds or it may be days before I hear the smallest noise, like the sound of a door being opened and closed. I stiffen. "Did you hear that?" I ask.

"What?" Marc says, still kissing me.

"The door."

Marc twists on top of me, and then moves back to kissing me. "It's shut," he says, and then I feel his fingertips brush underneath the hem of my shirt.

"Hey," I say, pushing them back. "Hey."

"Hey," he whispers, pushing his lips onto mine.

His hands are cold across my belly. His hips push into me. I can feel that he's excited, and it scares me. I feel as if I can't breathe. I feel as if I'm starting to think clearly.

His fingers are moving everywhere, up over my rib cage and underneath my bra. His hands cup my breasts. He presses his palms in gentle circles over my soft mounds.

"Stop," I whisper against his lips, not trusting myself, not trusting him. "Stop."

I feel my hips wiggle, push up against his. His hand lifts up the waistband of my skirt, slips silently underneath. His fingers brush the top of my panties.

"No," I twist underneath him. "Stop. I mean it."

"Huh?" he murmurs; his mouth nuzzles my neck.

"Stop," I say, arching up to kiss him.

"Okay." He sighs, burying his face in the pillow, moaning. "Okay," he repeats and then he rolls off me.

"Are you mad?" I ask, afraid to look at him.

"No." He grabs my hand, settles it into the curve of his chest. "I'm not mad." He closes his eyes.

A few minutes pass. I'm not sure what to do. I want to take my hand back, readjust my clothes, wipe the hair from my lips, and then sneak silently off to the bathroom to throw up. But I don't. I can't because that would be mean. So I lie there with Marc. But I think about Danny.

# THIRTY-TWO

# big fat liar

. . .

at school the next day, i try to do anything but think. my body aches. My head hurts. I can't seem to drink enough bottled water. I'm completely incapable of putting any sentences together. When Mr. Murphy pulls me aside to talk after class, I can barely look him in the eye. I feel like if anyone can see what's going on, it'll be Mr. Murphy.

"Susie, I spoke to Danny's mother this morning, and she's extremely happy with his progress." Mr. Murphy clears his throat and beams down at me. "So am I. You've done a really great job."

"Thanks," I say, but my head heats up. Ever since last night with Marc, all I can think about is Danny. I feel so guilty about Danny. I don't deserve Mr. Murphy's praise. I deserve a nice kick in the ass. "Is that it?" I don't mean to be short with Mr. Murphy. I just want to stop talking about Danny.

"Actually, no." Mr. Murphy shakes his head, surprised by my curtness. "I had a talk with Danny during our class earlier and we both agree that tutoring is no longer necessary. He thinks he can do it on his own."

"On his own?" Tutoring time is the only time that Danny and I spend alone. If he doesn't want me to tutor him anymore, does that mean he doesn't want to see me anymore? Was Danny using Mr. Murphy to break up with me?

"I know," Mr. Murphy says, mistaking my shock for disappointment. "But you've done a great job. I'm sure that I can find you someone else to tutor."

"Oh, yeah." I shrug and look down at the carpet. The same piece of gum from early October stares back at me. The two-minute-warning bell rings, and students from his next period start flooding in. "I have to go."

"Okay." Mr. Murphy moves aside to let two students with ridiculously large backpacks pass. "I'll see you tomorrow."

"Yeah, tomorrow," I say, wondering how I can even think of tomorrow when I'm not sure if I can make it through today.


it gets worse from there. in driver's ed, bobby and luis are absent. "They're at some geeky-ass bowling semifinals," José tells me. "Oh," José says, smiling at me, his eyes so red I can barely see his irises. "And watch out for Jessica. I hear she wants to kick your ass."

"Huh?" Instinctively, my head swivels in Jessica's direction. She's standing on the opposite side of the paved driver's range talking to Brianna Rivera, another bubble-headed cheerleader. She doesn't look happy. She's waving her arms around, and suddenly they both stop talking and look at me. Brianna shoots me the finger and Jessica gives me the dirtiest look I've had all year.

"What'd I do?" I ask José.

José chuckles and looks at me. "Shit. Are you kidding me?"

"What'd I do?" I repeat.

"Ask Tamara," he says, walking away.

I sit down in our squad line, not really sure what to do. I wait for

Coach Brown to come in, blow his whistle. Class doesn't start until he hits the pavement. I look around and see Tamara in a corner talking to Stan Levy and some other kids. She whispers something in his ear, and then they both look at me. Tamara smiles, but her smile says, *screw you*, and after a few minutes, she starts talking to another group of kids. Again, they all stop to look at me. Tamara gives me the fake smile. Then a few minutes later, she walks off and hits another group. Something is definitely up.

When the late bell rings, Coach Brown pulls up in his golf cart. "Let's go," he screams. He looks around the class, and notices that it's half empty.

"Where is everyone?" he asks Jessica, because she's closest to him.

"At a nerd convention," she replies, and he chuckles. She tosses her glossy black hair and smiles up at him. "The bowling geeks are bowling in a semifinal or something and the D.A.R.E. kids are on a field trip."

"Oh," Coach says. "Well, I'll guess we'll just pair up today, and each group will get a car. Get into your squads."

We all line up in our squads. José first, Jessica behind him, Tamara behind her, and me in the back. Our line is filled with tons of tension, except for José, who appears to be finding the whole situation amusing because he keeps laughing and mumbling "catfight" underneath his breath.

"Shut up," Jessica hisses before slapping him on the back of his head.

The coach works his way down the squad, breaking each squad into groups of two. When he gets to us, he puts José with Jessica. I get stuck with Tamara.

"Thank God," Jessica snaps at the both of us and then runs to catch up with José, punching him in the arm when she gets next to him.

Tamara and I walk quietly to our car. She gets the driver's seat. I get the passenger side with its funny emergency foot brake.

"So," Tamara says, after she throws the car in drive, "some memorial service." She gives me a sidelong glare that makes my body fill with dread. She knows.

Still I say, "What's that supposed to mean?"

Tamara laughs, turning the steering wheel right and pulling to a stop at a fake stop sign. "You know what I mean."

"No," I tell her, making sure to keep my voice level. "I don't."

"Yes," she says, not even bothering to look at me, "you do."

We drive, passing fake stop sign after fake stop sign. Tamara stops for the pedestrian crosswalk, the blinking yellow light, the careful-or-they'll-get-you intersection. She keeps her perfectly manicured nails at ten and two. At the parallel-parking station, I hit the emergency foot brake and the car comes to a crashing halt. I have to know.

"Who'd you tell?" My voice comes out in little gasps.

She laughs and hits my leg so hard that the emergency foot brake is released. "Everyone."

"Even Danny?" I ask.

But she doesn't reply. She gives me a wicked smile, but she doesn't reply.


at lunch, i run to my spot and contemplate sitting there for the rest of the day, possibly for the rest of my life. Today Marisol is eating lunch with Ryan. She didn't even tell me that she was going to. I found out as I was passing the cafeteria. It doesn't surprise me. Nothing else can surprise me today.

Danny finds me with my head shoved deeply into my hands, the uneaten contents of my bagged lunch spread out on the newly cut grass. I don't look up to let him know that I know that he is there, because if I did then I am sure that he would see that I've been crying.

"You okay?" He sits down next to me.

"Yep." I turn my face away, wiping my tears with the back of my hand. I can't be any more obvious, I know. But I don't really have a choice.

"You don't look okay."

"I am."

"You're crying," he points out.

"I know." I'm smart enough to know that there's no point in denying it. "It's okay."

"Is it?"

"Danny," I blurt out quickly, "are we—" I stop myself. I was going to ask, *Are we a couple?* Because if we're not, then what I did last night with Marc can't technically be considered cheating. Right? But if we *are* a couple . . .

"Are we what?" His voice drops. I wonder if he knows. *Can I still spin this?* I think. Then I wonder, *When did I become the type of girl that spins things?*

"Why are you here?" I change tactics.

"I thought I'd find you here." He picks at a blade of grass and breaks it apart in his fingers. "I thought maybe we could go back to my house. You know . . ." his voice trails off.

"You mean not go back to school?"

"Yeah," he says after a while.

"Danny," I push the breath from my lungs. Before I say yes to his house, I have to know. "Are we . . . together?"

He picks another blade of grass, twists it into a knot but doesn't answer.

"Danny . . ."

"Yeah," he says slowly.

"Oh."

"Do you want to go back to my house?" he asks again. He stands, holds his hand out to me, doesn't look me in the eyes.

"Yeah." I take his hand. And then without another word, I follow him home.

as i enter danny's home, i can't help but think that besides crossing the threshold of his door, I have crossed several other thresholds.

In the space of three months, I have become that girl who:

1. Skips school.

2. Gets drunk at her mother's memorial service.

3. Makes out with the pothead next door.

4. Fights with her best friend.

The weird thing is that I've never felt so normal.

"Do you want something to drink?" Danny opens the refrigerator, turns an inquisitive eye toward me.

"No." I lift up my water bottle. "I'm fine."

"You sure?" He reaches deep in the back and pulls out a long brown bottle with a silver label. "Bud Light," he says, holding it out to me. "Take it."

"I don't drink," I say, my heart pounding in my ears.

"Oh." He gives me a funny look. "Okay."

Danny puts the beer back in the refrigerator and grabs a Capri Sun. He sits on the counter and looks at me intently. "So . . ." he says, kicking the cabinets hard with his feet, "what'd you do last night?"

Even though I know that he knows, my mind tells me to act like he doesn't. Or at least to act like I have no idea what he's talking about. I know it's crazy, but I feel trapped and I'm not sure why I let myself walk right into it.

Still, I struggle with what to tell him. At the very least, I should tell him about my mother's memorial service. I should try to explain the story so that it works out in my favor and not in Tamara's. Because that's obviously how he heard, right?

Still for whatever reason, I say, "Nothing."

"*Nothing?*" he repeats.

"*Nothing,*" I mumble, "that I want to talk about."

"*Okay.*" He hops off the counter and grabs my hand. "C'mon."

"Where?" I ask, digging my heels into the tile.

"To my bedroom, where else?" he asks, shaking his head strangely.

"You're acting weird," I tell him, but I let him pull me along. I can't seem to stop him.

"You're going to call me weird when you can't even tell me what you did last night?" He gives me a look that says, *You're the weirdo.*

"You know what?" I disengage my hand from his. I think I can still make a break for it, so I say, "I don't feel well. I have a headache. I'm going to go back to school." I turn quickly, grab my book bag off the counter, and head for the sliding glass door. Danny follows close behind, so I move faster.

"Why are you freaking out?" His voice is monotone, slightly bored.

"I'm not freaking out." I fumble with the lock on the sliding door. "I just have a really bad headache."

"Headache or hangover?" His voice catches speed. "Does Marc have a hangover, too?"

The question slams into me.

"What?" I ask against my better judgment. "What are you talking about?"

"Susie." He pushes up behind me, places his hands on my shoulders. "Don't lie to me. *Please.*"

I turn to face him. He's standing so close. Our chests are pressed against one another. I can feel every breath he takes.

"Back up," I say slowly.

He steps backward until he is sitting on his family room couch. I wait to speak, trying to judge what I should say. He sits with his head in his hands; his foot taps impatiently against the coffee table.

"Can I ask you a question?" The shift in his tone catches me off guard. He's back in control. "Are we . . . together?" He asks.

"What?" It's a question that apparently neither of us has the answer to.

"Are we together?" he repeats. "You asked me that earlier at the canal, and I want to know what you think." He pauses. "I really do want to know what you think."

"I don't know what to think," I tell him, rapping my head against the glass door. "I don't."

"I don't either." He looks away from me. I wonder if he'll ever really look at me again.

"Then what difference does it make?" I say quietly.

"What difference do I make?" he shoots back. "To you?"

"Danny," I whisper his name softly. "I . . . I like you. A lot." Telling him that I like him is one of the hardest things that I've ever had to say, but I say it anyway because I understand that I might never have the opportunity to say it again.

"But, Susie, what difference does it make if you like me, if you can't tell me anything? Why didn't you tell me about your mom's memorial service?" He takes a deep breath. "Why didn't you at least tell me about Marc?"

How could I tell him about Marc? To tell him about Marc so that he would understand, I would have to tell how most of the time I walk around like I'm carrying twenty rocks on my shoulders. How sometimes the anxiety is so bad that I just want to disappear. That until I met him, I was able to push all these feelings away, hide behind my Blockbuster card, my silly little life where nothing ever changed. How can I tell him all that? I barely understand it myself.

"I just couldn't." I slide down the glass door and bury my head in my knees to hide the tears.

"You should go." He walks over to me, gives me his hand to help me up. I take it, knowing that it's probably the last time we'll ever touch.

"Okay." I stand. I feel him looking at me, but I keep my head close to my body. I don't want him to see me.

He pushes the sliding glass door open and waits for me to leave. But now I don't want to leave; I want to stay.

"What about tutoring?" I ask, all sense of pride gone. "You have that big test on Friday."

"I already told Mr. Murphy that I don't need you to tutor me anymore," he says. "But don't worry, I've already found someone else to help."

"Who?" I push the tears back and look up at him, but somehow, I already know. We both know that I already know.

"Susie—" he says.

"No, who?" I ask again. I want to hear him say it.

"Tamara. It's Tamara."


after i leave danny's house, i don't go home. i wander aimlessly around the canal, thinking about the last few months of my life.

At the far end of the canal, fifteen houses away from Danny's, I sit down underneath a tree. Ironically, the weather is nippy today. Still, not having the sun beat down on my head makes me feel better. The grass is soft beneath my body and I just want to curl up in a fetal position and cry . . . so I do.

Lying on the grass with my eyes closed, I remember what it was like to kiss Danny. And then I think about Marc. I think about how it felt to have his body over mine, how I liked it—how I wanted him to be Danny. And then I think about Danny back at his house. I think about our bodies pressed together, feeling his chest rise, feeling his breath enter his body.

And then I think about my dad and how we never talk about my mom. How she stopped existing in words the day that she died. I tried once when I was in sixth grade. I asked him if he missed her. I missed her. I think I just wanted someone to really, really understand. But all he did was sigh. He looked down at me, his eyes so weary, his head turned into the refrigerator and he sighed. I stood there waiting, my feet cold from the tile. I waited. And the waiting turned into weeks, months, and then years. I think even now, I am still waiting.

# THIRTY-THREE

# dad starts to wake up

that night i walk home in the dark. when i get there all the lights are on, and Leslie's car is parked next to my father's. I stick my key in the lock and take a deep breath. I look like crap. I'm just hoping that nobody will point it out.

The minute I open the door, all hell breaks loose. My dad is screaming. Leslie is shaking her head. Marisol is sitting at the dining room table staring at me, totally confused.

"Where have you been?" my dad asks, his voice several decibels higher than I've ever heard it before. "Where have you been? I nearly called the police. It's nine o'clock!"

"Why didn't you?" I ask. I'm so tired, more tired than I've ever been in my entire life.

"Where were you?" he repeats.

"C'mon, Dad, you barely notice that I'm here when I'm here. What does it matter if I'm a few hours late? I'm home. I'm alive. Deal with it." I give him a dirty look and try to step around him, which is hard because he's intentionally blocking my path. All I want to do is go to my bed and never leave it.

"Where are you going? We're not done talking." He's furious. I don't blame him. I just don't care.

"I'm tired. I want to go to sleep. We'll talk about this in the morning." My voice is cold. Adult and cold.

"Susie," my dad asks again, blocking my path, "where have you been? Your school called. They said you missed every class after lunch. They said this is the second time you've done that."

"Move," I tell him quietly.

"No," he says, the heat from his breath pushing against my face. "This is my house. I asked you a question."

"I don't have to tell you." I move to the right, but he grabs my arm and holds me in place.

"Yes, you do. If you want to live here you do."

"Why are you acting like this? Why are you making this such a big deal? I want to go to sleep!" I yell.

"Why am I acting like this?" He grabs my shoulders and shakes me roughly. For the first time I notice that his eyes are redder than usual. His hair is all mussed up. "Why? *Susie*, don't you know what can *happen* to you out there?" His voice catches. He looks away from me.

"No, Dad, I don't know what can happen out there. I only know what can happen in here, which," I say, my voice spilling out of me with absolutely no control whatsoever, "is you ignoring me for the last six years and then freaking out on me because I'm a few *hours* late!"

"Where were you?" he repeats for the third time, but now the question is even less important to me than it was five minutes ago.

"None of your business." I try to untangle myself from him.

"Where?" His grip hardens.

"At. The. Canal." I practically spit each word into his face.

"Why didn't you call me? I didn't know where you were." He squeezes my shoulders so hard, I yelp in pain.

"Dad, you're hurting me." Once again, I try to pry myself away from him, but he won't let go. "Dad!" I scream at the top of my lungs. "You're hurting me!"

I was shaking now, my eyes tearing up more from shock than pain. My father didn't TOUCH ME. My father didn't LAY HIS FINGERS ON ME.

Leslie steps forward, places her hand over my dad's until she feels his fingers loosen. "Joe," she says, her voice calm and in control, "she'll tell us when she's ready. Okay? Maybe"—Leslie takes a step back, gives us some room—"we should all sit down and talk about this."

"I don't want to talk about this, Leslie. I want to go to my room."

"Susie," Marisol says, "come on."

"Oh shut up," I snap at Marisol. Where was she today when I needed her? And now she thought she could just come into my house and gang up on me? I don't think so. "What do you care? Do you know how bad school was for me today? Do you?" I take two steps closer to her, so that I'm staring down at her.

"What are you talking about?" She shakes her head at me. "Why do you always have to make things so difficult?"

"I'm not *making* anything difficult. Things are difficult for me *because that's just how it is.* But you wouldn't know that because you're too busy with your head stuck up your boyfriend's ass!"

"Susie." This time it's Leslie trying to calm me down. I can't stand the way these two think they can get me to do whatever they want because that's how it's been for the last six years.

"Look, Leslie"—my voice drips with sarcasm—"I'm just trying to go to sleep. I'm tired. We don't always have to talk about our feelings."

"Susie," Marisol says, her voice warning me, "don't talk to my mother like that."

"Well then, Marisol," I say in my bored voice, "please remind her that she's your mother and not mine."

"Why are you being such a bitch?" Marisol hisses.

"Because," I say rather simply, "I can."

"You know what?" Marisol says, standing up and walking to the door, "don't ever talk to me again. I'm tired of never having fun because of you, and always having to deal with your weird panic attacks, and always wondering if what I say is going to hurt your feelings." Her voice rises and reaches a plateau that is unsteady and wobbly.

"Yeah"—my voice grows higher, too—"well, I'm tired of you selling me out for Coldplay tickets, and lunch with Ryan, and for you not understanding that maybe, just maybe, on the day MY MOTHER DIED, I might not want to talk to YOU!"

"Yeah"—Marisol walks dangerously close to me—"well, I'm tired of your self-imposed drama. Making out with Marc on your DEAD MOTHER'S BED? How lame can you be?"

"What?" my father says. "What?"

"How do you know?" My voice rises up over my father's.

"Tamara told the whole school, okay?" Marisol shakes her head at me, like she's disappointed in me. "How could you hurt Danny like that?"

But my mind is thinking about something else. "You knew and you didn't try to find me?" Even Danny tried to find me. But my best friend left me out to dry.

Marisol looks away from me. She has nothing to say, and she can't meet my eyes.

"Girls." Once again Leslie takes control. "This is getting out of hand. Susie, I'm not sure what's going on with you, and you're right, I am not your mother. But I do love you, whether you like it or not."

Leslie pauses to exchange a look with my father. I stare at Marisol, still trying to comprehend on how many levels she has sold me out.

"Regardless," Leslie continues, "you had us worried. We didn't know what happened to you. And after losing your mother . . . You have to understand how that might make your dad feel. In the future, please call. Okay?"

I pull my eyes away from Marisol and turn to Leslie. I stare at her through slanted eyes. I wasn't here to take orders from her.

"Okay?" she repeats, offering me a shaky smile.

"Just shut up!" I tell her, the words ripping through my mouth like a tornado. "Just shut up with your okay bullshit! I'll never be okay!" I point at my dad. "He'll never be okay! We'll never be okay!"

I stop screaming, totally worn. I look at them. I look at each one of them, but nobody seems to be able to say anything. All they can do is stare at me, unsure of what to say or do next.

"I just want to go to bed," I mutter.

"Susie." My dad's voice is strained with anger. "What's going on with you? How dare you speak to Leslie like that?" He turns his back on me, and a loud moan seems to shake his entire body. "What is going on with you?"

"You want to know what's going on with me?" I say to his back. The back he has turned TO ME. And all I can think about is all the times I've tried to tell him about my life, my feelings, my thoughts, my fears, and I remember all the times that I've heard him say, "Maybe later," or "When this book is done," or "I promise it'll be soon." I remember all the empty promises that made me feel nonexistent, and I think how ironic it is that now—only now when we have an audience—he wants to know what's going on with me.

"Okay . . ." If he wants to know the truth, I'll give him the whole truth. "Let's see . . . In the last month Danny and I have skipped school, made out in the library, and slept together on the floor of his bedroom. Marc and I have mostly just talked, but he's been smoking a lot of pot, too. Then we got drunk, made out." I try to stop the words, hold on to my breath because what I am about to say can never be taken back, but the words keep coming. They want to get out. "Oh, you're going to love this one, Dad. I let him feel me up on Mom's bed. How's that?" I finish, a crazy person's smile splayed across my face.

I don't see the slap coming. I barely see Leslie jumping between us to prevent the second strike. But later in bed, I rub my jaw and stare in the mirror at the red circle that stains the right side of my face. I feel the sudden sting of it over and over again. And then, and only then, do I understand that I have gone too far.

# THIRTY-FOUR

# the aftermath

• • •

to be honest, i'm not really surprised when my dad grounds me for two months. It seems that's the least that he can do to assert his parental control.

And believe me, my dad is definitely asserting his parental control. According to his written set of instructions, I am to go to school, come home, do my homework, and go to sleep. I am not to do any extracurricular activities. I am not to speak to Marc. I am, basically, only allowed to breathe. Oh, and on good days, I can smile. But not too much.

Despite my wrecked home life, high school continues. As usual, nobody speaks to me, especially Marisol. Instead, we find an amicable way to dissolve our friendship. Basically, Marisol leaves me a note asking me to remove all of my things from HER locker. Then she leaves me a combination lock for my new locker. (Isn't that thoughtful?) And then, I carve some choice adjectives on the inside of HER locker. And our friendship, and any ties to that friendship, officially cease to exist.

As for Danny, he seems to have disappeared. I go days and days without ever seeing him. But I miss him. I miss the way his Zest smell. I miss the curls that fall into his eyes. I miss what had almost been and what will never be. Out of all the different parts of my life that I have chosen to no longer think about, Danny is the hardest to erase.

Oddly enough, Marc once again becomes my best friend. In the days following my breakup with Marisol and Danny, we spend a lot of school time together. Sometimes I talk. Sometimes he talks. Sometimes I listen. Sometimes he listens. Sometimes there is absolutely nothing to say, which is okay. I think we both just really don't want to be alone.

"So your dad must be super-pissed," Marc says, a few days after THE INCIDENT (which is how I refer to my father's slap in the face), "to keep up with your grounding like that. My mom never remembers when she grounds me."

We are eating lunch in a legendary OG "smoker's spot" outside one of the stairwell doors.

"Yeah, I think he's pretty pissed." More than pissed. My dad is so mad at me, he's barely looked at me for the last three days.

"Did you tell him about us?" Marc asks.

"Yep."

"Aw, shit, you know he's going to tell my mom." Marc looks only slightly worried. "Not that she'll care. Caring," he says, "might cause her to get some wrinkles and she's not into that. Any word on when you'll get off the hook?"

"None. I don't care. It's not like I have anywhere to be after school. Nobody to see. In case you haven't noticed, I'm kind of a loner."

"Nothing wrong with being a loner," Marc says, looking at me.

"Yeah." I pick at the edge of my pizza. "Except it gets lonely."

"Well . . ." Marc pulls out a cigarette and sniffs it. He dangles it from the side of his mouth while he searches for his lighter. "I don't know what to tell you. Smoke?" he says, when he finally gets it lit.

"You know I don't smoke." I push it away.

"I know. I'm hoping you'll change your mind." He blows the smoke in my face and smiles.

"Not on your life. So," I say, because the conversation is running thin.

"So," he says, flicking his cigarette away. "Come here."

"Why?"

"'Cause." He grabs my knee and drags me closer.

"Hey." I shove him away. "I'm still eating."

"No, you're not." He grabs my pizza and tosses it in the general vicinity of his cigarette. Then he finds the spot on my body, my childhood ticklish spot (the one right underneath my breast) and digs in. I crack up.

"No, fair. Stop!" I twist and turn, laughing hysterically. "Da—" I catch myself before I say it. "Just stop. Okay?"

"What did you say?" His arms fall to his sides.

"What?" I huff, out of breath. "I said stop!"

"No. You almost called me Danny."

Suddenly, I feel the pressure of his hand on my thigh.

"Oh."

"That's okay. I know you like Danny. I still like Sheila. It doesn't matter to me." He squeezes my thigh. "I guess that's just the way it is. Interesting, huh?" Marc sighs. "So, you're not supposed to be talking to me, huh?"

"No, I'm not." A change in subject is good. "I think, technically, the only other teenager that I'm allowed to talk to is me."

"So then we shouldn't talk." Marc rests his hands on my hips.

"What? Why not?"

"We should do this." Marc brushes his lips across mine. "Right?" Marc whispers into my ear. "This isn't talking, right?"

"No," I whisper back. "This is the opposite of talking." I wait for him to kiss me again. All I want is to not think about anything, and it seems to me that kissing is the perfect and only way to do that.

Even if it's kissing Marc.

. . .

185

about a week after THE INCIDENT, i give up hope that my dad is going to apologize. Or as I preferred to imagine, drop to his knees and beg my forgiveness.

Even without the apology, he lets me know how he feels. For starters, he:

1. Starts policing me—He leaves the door to his study open all the time. He checks his watch whenever I come and go. And because I'm mostly only allowed to come and not go, it isn't very often. But still, it's a new habit.

2. Stops seeing Leslie—For a week after THE INCIDENT, there were a ton of calls between the two of them and then the calls stopped. Like that.

3. Locks my mother's bedroom door. I noticed it immediately. The day after THE INCIDENT, I went to her room because I wanted to take a nap on her side of the bed and when I turned the doorknob, the door didn't budge. It was locked.

There are other small changes. Like when I get home from school, he actually comes out of his study to talk to me. And he listens to what I have to say—mostly. Which is huge.

Maybe he's looking for clues, pieces of my day where I've disobeyed his rules and regulations. Like, am I still talking to Marc? (Or making out with him in the smoking areas at school?) Am I cutting class? (Or taking restroom passes in driver's ed and conveniently forgetting to return them until five minutes before the dismissal bell?) Maybe he wants to bust me, so he talks to me, hoping I'll implicate myself in silly school scandals.

Or maybe something else is happening? I'm not sure. I don't care what his reasons are. All I know is that something IS happening. My father's finally waking up.

Thank God.

# THIRTY-FIVE

# marc

* * *

"you know, you do this little thing with your nose when you get mad."

"I do not." I shake my head, but it's true.

"Yes, you do." Marc brushes sand off his hand. "What's up?"

"Nothing," I reply automatically. I roll onto my back and stare at the sky. I love the beach during December.

"You're worried about skipping class," he says.

"No," but the truth is I am partially upset about skipping—again. It seems like all Marc and I do is miss more and more class. I'm running out of excuses to tell my teachers. You can say you've gotten your period only so many times before they get suspicious. So why am I here?

"I shouldn't have left. I only had two classes left. I could have stuck it out."

The thing is that school has become completely unbearable for me. Still, I can't afford to miss any more school. If Marc were a better friend, he'd know that.

"Yep," Marc said. "But how's that fun?"

"Do you always have to be fun?" I ask, annoyed with him.

"No, I just have to be invisible. I can't be invisible if I'm present. That's why I'm here."

And that's why we're friends. Ever since Marc and Sheila broke up, Marc wants to be invisible, just like me.

"I'm invisible," I tell him sarcastically, "yet somehow you always manage to find me."

"Of course." He scoots next to me and wraps the blanket from the back of his pickup truck over my body.

"Is this thing even clean?" I ask grumpily.

"Yep," he says, "as clean as the back of my truck."

Underneath the blanket, he wraps his arms around my waist. He buries his face in my neck. His stubble brushes along my cheekbone. It kind of hurts. I twist my head away, but Marc misinterprets my movement as interest. He blows an air bubble on my skin. In his own way, I guess he's being sweet, but all I can think of is that I hate the smell of his cigarette breath. With the blanket wrapped so tightly around us, I feel as if I am about to suffocate. And that feeling makes me want to scream, *What am I doing here with you? What am I doing with my life?* But of course I don't. Instead I say, "Do you ever pretend that I'm Sheila?"

His back straightens, and I feel like telling him to forget the question.

"You don't have to say, if it makes you feel uncomfortable."

"I don't pretend you're anything. Do you pretend that I'm Danny?"

"But you miss Sheila?" I ask, avoiding his question.

"Yeah, kind of. But you know that." He scoots a little bit away from me. "Maybe we shouldn't talk about this."

"Why not?"

"You know, you're really making me glad that I invited you here."

He pulls out a cigarette and attempts to light it, but the wind blows it out. "Fuck, this wind bites."

"You smoke too much anyway," I tell him.

"Yep, and you complain too much." He pulls the covers over his head and seconds later emerges with a lit cigarette.

I stare at him, and it suddenly becomes apparent that at this moment we officially don't like each other. Not like we keep trying to pretend that we do.

"I think we should go," I tell him standing.

"I think I just got here," he says without budging.

"Well, I want to go. I want to go, Marc," I tell him louder.

"Fine," he says, but he doesn't stand up. He couldn't care less. "Fine, let's go. I'll take you back to school. What with traffic it'll take us about an hour to get back and then school will pretty much be over. But I'll take you back because that's what you want. Right, Susie?" His voice is monotone.

I sit back down. It frustrates me that he's right. "Fine," I tell him. "We'll stay."

"Good. Fuck, this cigarette went out again." He pulls the cover over his head and once again emerges with the cigarette lit. "This wind really bites."

"You smoke too much anyway," I tell him again.

"And you," he says with a sarcastic nod of his head, "complain too much."

# THIRTY-SIX

# the other holidays

●　●　●

on christmas day, my parole officer and i visit my grand-parents. My grandfather has prepared one juicy, but dead turkey, plenty of homemade mashed potatoes and gravy, yams smothered with marshmallows, corn on the cob, stuffing, and three different types of pies. My grandmother had also done some hard work that day. She made Jell-O-rama. My father and I are almost afraid to see it, but she insists that we both have a slice.

"I'm kind of full," I tell my grandmother. "I'm really stuffed."

"What a coincidence," my dad chimes in, "me, too."

"Okay, okay," my grandmother laughs. She has no clue who we are. She's been doing the *I see dead people* thing all day. "They don't want the Jell-O-rama," she tells her dead father. She laughs again, and I feel sorry for her. Even though it's absolutely disgusting with its wobbly green body and chunks of Snickers bars, marshmal-lows, and Reese's Pieces, it's still what she spent the entire day work-ing on.

"I'll take a slice, Grandma. There's always room for Jell-O-rama. Right, Dad?" I kick him hard underneath the table.

"Right, *Daughter*." He shoots me a dirty look, and for the first time in nearly a month, we aren't exchanging glares.

"Good." She hops off her chair and skips to the counter to retrieve her cake knife, which is surprising. I mean, that someone in her condition would be allowed to handle a knife. But whatever.

"Are you really going to eat that?" my dad whispers while she's gone.

"Yes, and so are you," I tell him with a wicked smile. "Every last piece."

"Okay." He slumps in his seat and loosens his belt. "You know, I really am full."

"Save it for someone who cares. You're eating it."

"Fine," he says, accepting my challenge. "You win."

"Finally." I half expect him to glare at me in disapproval.

"Finally," he repeats and then lowers his head, the corner of his lips reaching what might almost be considered a grin.

despite the smile, my parole officer and i drive home in silence. The radio is on but the volume is off. The lights behind us burn a hole in the rearview mirror that my father isn't using. Tonight, he's driving on autopilot. Not surprising.

I sneak a glance at the backseat and marvel at how we were able to fit all my gifts into the car. My grandfather went overboard this year, and probably maxed his JCPenney card in the process.

I let my hair down and press my head as far as I can into my headrest. I imagine that if I press really hard, my head might disappear and then I won't have to see the look of defeat splashed across my father's profile.

Rain shimmies down my window pane, and I try to recount all the things about my grandmother that I can remember. I remember the way she called teenagers "teeny boppers." How an ankle bracelet meant you were headed for a life of prostitution. How she ran my grandfather in circles if he didn't follow her advice. These are the pieces of my grandmother that are being erased. And they're the pieces that we all miss.

when we get home, i head straight for my bedroom. my head is throbbing. I want to talk to someone, anyone besides my dad. I debate calling Marc, but lately things have been pretty uncomfortable between us.

"I want to show you something." My dad flicks my bedroom light on.

"Dad, I just want to go to sleep."

"I know." My dad stares down at me curled up on my bed. "I'm tired, too." He pauses, like, forever. "You know, Susie, I'm aware that I don't understand you. I thought that if I stayed strong, that would be enough for you, which," he says, seeing my quizzical look, "doesn't make any sense.

"I'm not sure if anything I've done in the last six years makes sense. I don't remember half of it. I get up. I get dressed. I wake you up. I work. I write. Those are the five things that I committed myself to managing. Everything else seemed unimportant." His entire body sighs. "Susie, I'm sorry."

He's at the door. His hand presses against the plate of the light switch. His breath is shallow. His shoulders shake, the way a tree shakes when a storm is approaching. I'm not sure if I want to stick around for this. I want to leave, but I don't. I sit on my bed and watch. I watch as he becomes a mirror of what I feel inside. And it's hard as hell, because I'm so scared. I'm so scared.

"I'm sorry," he says, coming to me, sitting with me, rocking me. "I'm so very sorry."

"It's not your fault," I whisper, eager to forgive him.

"But it is," he says into my hair. "It is."

I stay silent. I'm not sure what to say. For a long time, I felt as if my father were as lost as my mother, as lost as my grandmother. But maybe the entire time he was lost, he was trying to be found? Maybe I had never noticed. I had never noticed because I had been so lost, too.

we sit in my room, holding each other. for the most part, i feel small and fragile in my father's arms. I feel weightless—the lightness of being. After a while, I drift off. My head grows heavier and heavier. I try to stay awake. I do everything I can. I count the number of hairs that coat his forearm. But despite my determination, I fall asleep.

When I awake, there's light outside my window. My shoes are still on, and I immediately kick them off. I pull my hair tie out and place it on the table next to my bed, and that's where I find it—the tattered yellow notebook, my father's journal.

I pull it off the table and bring it close to me. I open the torn cover and start to read. It's there—all of it. My mom, my dad, me. I can't stop reading. I read the entire day. I absorb each word, lock it into my memory so that I'll never forget. I wear its essence like a mist over my skin. I read and I read until the words waver and laughter leaves a little kink in my stomach, which turns into a heartbreak that can't be described.

# THIRTY-SEVEN

# the missing

. . .

during the rest of my christmas vacation, i sit in my room, write songs, and think about Marisol and Danny. I start to separate myself from Marc. We don't hang out, not because I think that Marc has no place in my life, but because I know that the place he occupied doesn't belong to him. One day, I'll let him back in. But for now, I need to be alone.

The missing doesn't start suddenly. It's probably always been there. I know what it's like to miss people. I miss my grandmother every time I see her. I miss my mother every time I walk through the empty halls of our home. I miss her the most when I see her picture over the mantel in our living room or at night when I remember those moments when our breath shared the same space. Like I said, the missing has always been there. Only now, I am ready to face it. I'm ready to face everything.

Not being around Marisol is like being cut in half. She's the missing person with whom I have imaginary conversations. I tell her how my next-door neighbor Mr. Godfrey is out of control with his bronzing lotion. I tell her how my garden isn't living up to expectations now that it's chilly. I tell her why I cut out Marc and how I miss Danny. Even though Marisol isn't here, I still tell her everything.

Danny is different.

I don't talk to Danny. I guess that's because I didn't really talk to him that much when we were together. Danny is that guy. That guy who was almost my friend, almost my boyfriend, almost my every-thing. In my mind, that's the place that he'll occupy throughout the history of my life—my almost everything. Still, I miss him.

after christmas day, my father starts to open up to me. he's hesitant, I can tell.

"Did you read this book?" he asks one day.

"No."

"Good book," he says, "I really liked it. You should read it." He leaves the book on the table and walks away.

And then on another day he says to me, "I don't understand why they would offer tenure to a professor who's written seven books that are largely ignored by the mainstream because of their extreme ver-bosity."

And then the next day he says, "My editor is driving me crazy with these revisions."

Finally, we get to something important on New Year's Eve. "Do you miss Marisol?" he asks me.

We're sitting at the breakfast table, eating pancakes and sausage. My father has abandoned eating breakfast in front of the computer to make a rare early-morning appearance.

"Yes," I say.

"Me, too," he replies.

We stare at each other over our orange juice.

"Do you miss Leslie?" I ask him.

"Yes," he says rather bluntly.

"Oh." I go back to my pancakes.

"Does that bother you?" he asks a couple of minutes later.

"I don't know . . ." I respond slowly. "Maybe."

"Okay." He picks absently at the last of his sausage.

"We're not too good at this talking thing," he says, laughing.

"No," I tell him, smiling. "We're not, but we don't totally suck either."

"No, we don't suck," he agrees, and for that moment I love him completely.

"I love you, Dad," I blurt out.

"Yeah." He looks at me for a long moment. "I love you, too."

It's a funny thing when someone says something you've been waiting to hear for a good portion of your life. It's like suddenly it doesn't feel like it took so long for them to say it, because in some way you always knew that they meant to and eventually one day they would get around to it.

"Well, I better get back to those revisions." He stands up, but hesitates as though unsure if we still have more to say to one another.

"You can call Leslie," I tell him.

"Yeah. Are you sure?"

"Yes. I'm sure she'd like to hear from you on New Year's Eve," I tell him.

"And you? Are you going to call Marisol?"

Touché.

"I've tried that." And I have. I've been calling her all morning, but she hasn't picked up her phone. Damn Caller ID. "I think I'm going to have to apologize in person. But you go first."

He chuckles. "Okay, I'll do that." He shuffles down the hallway, whistling underneath his breath.

# THIRTY-EIGHT

# the invisible line

. . .

i don't wait long to go to marisol. nine hours and fourteen minutes to be exact. It's enough time to get my head together and debate exactly what my opening line should be. I think it has to be funny—something to break the tension. As silly as it sounds, I practice in front of the mirror. I try to find a thousand ways to say I'm sorry. Like with a British accent: "I came around to apologize for being such an utter cow. All right then, I'm glad we got that out of the way. Carry on."

And . . .

"What I meant to say was 'God bless you,' not 'I hate you.' Clearly, you can see how I could get those two sentences confused."

And . . .

"Of course, when you stand there and block the door to your house, I get the feeling that you don't want me here, but that would be me just being self-conscious, right? Right?"

And then . . .

"I'm sorry."

I settle on *I'm sorry*. Even so, it takes me two hours of twitchy hands and four anxiety-fueled bathroom breaks before I can force myself to leave for Marisol's.

The walk there is slow. I count each square of concrete sidewalk. I think about Danny. I think about Danny kissing me in the library. I think about how I would apologize to him. For some reason, thinking about Danny makes it easier to get to square number three hundred five—the one right in front of Marisol's house.

Okay, deep breath.

I ring the doorbell, try not to faint, and say a little prayer that Leslie will not answer the door.

She does. Of course.

"Susie?"

"Hi, Leslie." I have a hard time looking her in the eyes.

"Hey . . ." She smiles. It seems pretty genuine. "How have you been? We've missed you around here."

"I'm okay. Thanks." I wonder if I can slide under the doormat and hide there forever. I can be the invisible human skin that falls to the floor and gets trapped under her shoe. It'd be a lot easier than standing here.

"So . . ." Leslie says.

"So . . ."

And it's obvious that this is the point in the conversation where I explain to her why I walked three hundred five concrete blocks to land on her doorstep. But I don't. I stand there as an awkward pause turns into an awkward silence, and I tell myself that I can outlast her, totally forgetting that Leslie stays quiet for a living.

"Is Marisol home?" I ask finally.

"No. She's visiting her dad until tomorrow. He and his new wife wanted to spend some time with her."

"Steve got remarried? Wow." Marisol must be going crazy locked up in a three-bedroom condo on the beach with her dad and Barbie the inflatable stepmonster.

"Christmas Eve." Leslie shakes her head. "You know Steve. Every holiday has to be about him."

"Oh . . . Well . . . Can you tell her I stopped by?"

"Yes, I will."

"Thanks, well, I should go." I turn on my heel, regretting the fact that I hadn't worn my running shoes.

"Susie?"

"Yeah?" I turn back even though I want to go, go, go.

"Would you mind if we talked for a minute?"

"Okay . . ." I say, but all I can think is, *How many seconds are in a minute?*

"Why don't you come inside and we can talk?"

"Okay." I move through the doorway and stand stoically on the doormat.

"The couch, maybe?"

"Okay," I say. Again.

"You can sit, really. I won't change my mind." She nudges me down onto the couch.

"Sure." I laugh nervously. "Leslie—"

"Susie."

We stop, neither sure who should go first.

"Me first?" Leslie says.

"Okay."

"I know you loved your mother very much—"

"I *love* my mother very much," I interject.

"Yes, I'm sorry. You love your mother very much," she amends and nods before continuing. "And I know you love your father very much, too." She pauses to consider her words. "I don't want any of that to change. Is it possible that some part of you thinks that I do?"

She waits for me to answer, but I don't know what to say. The obvious response to that question would be no.

"No," I say.

"Good, because I don't."

"*Okay* . . ." I respond.

"I know it's hard to see your father interested in someone else romantically. I know that can be . . . difficult. And we can both agree that it's been a little difficult for you. Wouldn't you say that is true?"

She is good at her job. Obviously. She basically has me agreeing to everything she says. Still, I don't want to give in to this point. I don't know why. I just don't.

"I don't know," I tell her. "I haven't given it a lot of thought."

"Okay." She leans back a little and tilts her head. Her eyes dart back and forth like she's considering changing her tactics. "Do you know what it's like to be in love?" She leans forward and smiles at me.

"I don't know." I mean, I liked Danny a lot, but love? How can I know if I've been in love if I have nothing to compare it to?

"Well, do you know what it's like to get that bubble in your stomach when you're around a boy? Or to feel like you could burst into a hundred giggles after he speaks to you because you can't believe that you got to share five minutes of his time? Or do you know what it's like to think about that other person every minute of the day and wonder what he's doing, or what he's thinking about, or if he might, even for a second, be thinking about you?" She sighs deeply before continuing. "Well, that's love—more or less. There are other elements that are involved, like trust, fidelity, commitment, but that is the bare-bones definition of what love feels like."

"Oh," is all I can muster because I'm thinking. I'm thinking about Danny and that moment after Halloween. I'm thinking about Marc and those minutes on my mother's bed. It all seems very confusing to me—to pinpoint whether either experience could have amounted to love. Still, with Danny it seemed like there was a strong possibility.

"Well." Leslie's voice lures me back to the now. "Your father was in love with your mother—very much so. I can remember them at their ten-year anniversary party. He was so good to her—telling the story of how they met, their wedding day . . . when they found out that they were going to be parents. You could see it. You could see it in his eyes." Leslie's voice is soft. "He loved her."

"I know," I tell her. "I remember." And I do. I remember that party. I was only six, but I remember.

"Good. It's important that you never forget that." She takes a moment to collect her thoughts and then begins again. "But can you imagine feeling all of that . . . love . . . and then when that love is taken from you so abruptly . . . having to live with not only the loss of that love, but the knowledge that you will never feel it again? Can you imagine?"

Leslie waits for me to respond, but I can't because I'm imagining what that would mean. What would it mean to love someone the way my father loved my mother and then lose that? How does it feel to lose your wife—the person with whom you'd shared the last fifteen years of your life? I can't imagine. Suddenly, I realize that I have absolutely no clue as to the depth of my father's sorrow.

"Can you imagine?" Leslie repeats to my silence.

I know what it's like to lose my mother—that missing, that ache, that anger. All of those feelings, I know. But maybe, on some level, there is a greater pain. I saw how my father looked day after day. I saw the way he walked back and forth from his study. I saw how he wasn't really much for talking. He's a storyteller, but he never wants to tell his stories aloud—at least, not anymore. When my mother was alive, she used to beg him for a moment of silence. Now all we have is silence. Well, before New Year's Eve.

Why didn't I see this bigger picture? My father—a widower, a single parent, a person all alone with no one to talk to, no Marisol to confide in—with nothing but his writing and me. And then he almost had Leslie, and I had to take that away.

"No." I shake my head, defeated. "I can't imagine."

"No," she says after a few seconds of silence, "I doubt many of us can. I know that on many levels I certainly cannot."

"I really do want him to be happy," I tell Leslie, a searing pain suddenly gripping my chest. I don't want my father to sit around night after night stuck in his study, writing about a life that he used to have. I want him to live outside in the real world.

"I know," she tells me. Her hand pushes its way into mine. "I do, too."

a few hours later, i leave leslie's. we had an honest-to-goodness talk and it took quite a bit of time and a whole lot of tears, but as I count my way back home, I'm glad we had it.

Being in Leslie's house—I suddenly realize how much I miss it. I miss my Friday nights with Marisol, and my Saturday morning breakfasts as part of their family. I miss what we all used to have together. It's funny that I didn't miss it before, but I guess it was because I never realized that I had it before.

I used to think that my life sucked, but, now, after being excluded from the routine of my life, I realize that my life is pretty darn good. I have my father—as flawed as he is, but so am I. I have Leslie, and for a long time I had Marisol. She was the best friend I ever had.

"You tried to call Marisol?" Leslie asked before I left.

"Yeah." I called Marisol, but I never left a message. I didn't know what to say.

"I probably shouldn't say this, but it's been very hard for her not to call you."

"Really?"

"Yes. Now are you sure you don't want a ride home? It's dark, and your father might get worried."

"Just call him and tell him that I'm on the way."

"Okay," Leslie says, "I'll call him."

It was a good feeling to push Leslie back in my father's direction. As much as it will twist my insides to see my dad with someone other than my mother, I know that Leslie's good for him and me. He has to have an adult life, too.

Still, the thought of my dad and Leslie one day becoming . . . and Marisol living in my house . . . as much as I used to fantasize about that actually happening in some alternate universe, I never really wanted it to become true. And maybe it won't . . . if I'm lucky.

"You need a ride?"

I hear the *clunkity-clunk* of my father's car long before I hear his voice. I turn to look at him and smile through the dark. It's nice to see him caring, even if it was a long time coming.

"I'm okay. It's just a block away."

"You sure?"

"Yeah, Dad. But you can follow me home," I yell over my shoulder.

"Okay," he says. And he does. He follows me the entire block home.

# THIRTY-NINE

# sisters forever

. . .

at precisely eleven fifty-five p.m. that night the phone starts ringing, and it doesn't stop. It doesn't stop ringing, despite the fact that no one's picking it up. It doesn't stop ringing, despite the fact that I try really hard to ignore it by turning the TV volume up and snuggling farther into the fluffy cushions of my family room sofa.

No matter what I do, the phone does not stop ringing.

"Dad," I moan, but he doesn't hear me. He's passed out next to me on the sofa with his mouth dangling open. Mogley's going to town on him, licking cookie crumbs off his unsuspecting face.

It's been a strange New Year's Eve. After I got home from Leslie's, my father and I grabbed just about everything sugary from the kitchen cabinets and proceeded to eat it all as quickly as we could. Then we fell into a sugar coma on the sofa—half sleeping, half watching TV, half fighting to keep Mogley from making us his sofa bitch—and we haven't moved since. So far, it's been a night of pure bliss.

"Dad," I moan again, but I think he's gone for good, because Mogley's French-kissing him, and he's not even stirring.

"Fine." I stretch my body over the coffee table, grab the phone by the cord, and clumsily toss it to my ear, all the while bracing myself for Aunt Emily's irritating, high-pitched shriek.

But I don't get Aunt Emily's "Happy New Year!" Instead, I get this: "Susie, why haven't you called me? Do you know what a nightmare I'm living? Do you have any freaking idea?"

"Marisol?" I think the sugar may have glued my mouth shut, because it's hard to get it open, and once I do get it open, I can barely squeak out her name. "Marisol? Is that you?"

"*Hello?* Who'd you think it was? Aunt Emily?"

"Well, yeah." I struggle to sit up. My head's pretty foggy. "Why are you calling me?"

"Why am *I* calling *you?*" She's still screaming, and I have to hold the phone away from my ear just so I don't go deaf. "Why aren't *you* calling *me?*"

"No, that's not what I mean. I—" I shake my head clear so that I can remember everything that I want to say to her to make things better. I take so long that Marisol starts singing, "Hello? Hello?" on the other side of the line.

"I'm here."

"Well?" Marisol snaps.

"I wanted to call you the minute I got home from talking to your mom, but I didn't have your dad's phone number, and I didn't know how to get ahold of you, and then I thought, well, maybe it's better if we talk in person, and I knew you were coming home tomorrow . . ." My voice trails off, even though I don't mean for it to.

"And?" Marisol says, although she's no longer yelling or snapping.

"And—" And now that I'm going, the words start flying out of my mouth. "What I meant to say is *why* would you call me after all the terrible things that I said to you? I was horrible. I was really, really mean."

"Yeah." Marisol sighs loudly. "I know. I was there."

"So . . ." I'm not sure if I should ask it, but I do anyway. "Why are *you* calling *me?*"

There's a long lull, and I wonder if Marisol's hung up on me. Maybe I shouldn't have asked the question again, maybe I should have gone straight to the begging part of the conversation, maybe I should have—

"Susie—"

*Oh, good. She's still there.*

"Susie, I talked to my mom, and she told me what you said to her, and I want you to know that I'm sorry, too. I never . . ." She trails off for a second. "I never knew what you were going through, and I'm sorry that I didn't try harder to understand."

She was apologizing to me? She was sorry?

"But I'm the bitch," I say, without thinking. "You never have fun because of me!"

"I have fun with you!" Marisol practically shouts. "I have so much fun with you. I have fun watching movies and pigging out and having slumber parties. *What, are you crazy?* But I *also* want to go out on dates and see concerts and do other stuff, outside the house. Don't you want to try that stuff, too?"

If Marisol had asked me this same question a few months ago, I would have definitely said, *No, absolutely not, NEVER.* But now I wanted to try to change. I wanted to try to be different. I wanted to try to be better.

"Yeah, I do want that stuff, too."

"You do?" Marisol sounds surprised. "Really? Seriously? 'Cause I want to do stuff like that with you, but I don't want you to feel like you have to do stuff like that with me just so we can be friends—"

"Marisol, I'm serious. I want to, and not for you, for me. I don't want to live my life in a box anymore."

We're quiet. My eyes wander over to sleepy Dad, only he's not sleeping anymore, and I nearly drop the phone, when I see that he's watching me, smiling.

"So, can I call you tomorrow?" I ask Marisol.

"No," Marisol says, but she doesn't sound mean.

"No?" And even though she doesn't sound mean, and I think she's joking, my voice still quivers.

"No, don't call me," Marisol laughs. "Come over. I'll be home by three, and bring your stuff. You're spending the night. You will not believe the stories I have to tell you. I'll give you two clues: Inflatable stepmonster from hell and stripper pole."

"Oh, Marisol—" I can't help it, I giggle.

"You have no idea. So, tomorrow?"

"Yeah," I smile, "tomorrow."

"And Susie—"

"Yeah?"

"Happy New Year."

"Happy New Year to you, too, Marisol."

After I hang up the phone, I look back at my dad and he's grinning like a goofball.

"What?" I give him a look. Just how much of the conversation did he hear?

"Nothing." He shakes his head and wipes at his face. I wonder if he knows that Mogley just finished making out with him. "I'm just proud of you."

"Yeah?"

"Yeah," he says, hugging me. "I really am."

# FORTY

# an intervention

. . .

the first wednesday back, mr. murphy asks me to stop by his classroom after school to talk about possibly tutoring another one of his students, a sophomore named Rebecca Johnson.

At first I'm not really sure about the whole thing. I mean, I tutored Danny and look what a total disaster that turned out to be. (Although, maybe it wasn't so much of a disaster because Mr. Murphy tells me that Danny is doing really well, and I refuse to give thousand-watt Tamara any credit for that. That was my doing, even if Danny doesn't want to remember that it was.) But Mr. Murphy gives me a hundred reasons why I should tutor again, so it's no surprise that I find myself outside his door later that afternoon.

What is a surprise is when I go to enter Mr. Murphy's classroom, I look through the Plexiglas window and see Danny sitting in the front row, tapping his feet against his chair, writing something.

The thing is I can't believe my eyes—because they're blinking so rapidly that my vision is blurring; or my heart—because it's officially having a heart attack; or my ears—because they're ringing the alarm;

or any other part of my body—because I've gone limp, even though the only thought in my cowardly head is, *RUN! RUN! RUN!*

And that's exactly what I intend to do, except when I turn, using stealth only a ninja could execute, I run smack-dab into Mr. Murphy's chest, hitting his fuzzy green cashmere sweater with the full force of my face.

"Oh." It's a hard hit, and it pushes Mr. Murphy back two steps before he can recover. "Susie." Without missing a beat, he looks down at his watch. "Perfect timing. How did your literature meeting go?"

I find it hard to talk, so I stutter and it goes something like this: "Er, um, go-go-good."

"Wonderful." He claps his hands together and smiles down at me. Why is he always so cheery? Is it that he's crazy (in a good way) or just really, really happy?

But does this really matter? I have to go. I have to get out of here. I have to—

And that's when I hear the door creep open behind me, and I know that Danny is standing right behind me.

"Oh," Danny says, and then his voice changes so that there's no sound of surprise left in it. "Mr. Murphy?" And I see his arm, his chocolate-skinned arm, hand a paper past me. And I see that it's clearly marked *The Picture of Dorian Gray—Makeup Essay*. He says, "I'm finished."

Mr. Murphy takes the essay and smiles at the both of us. "Wonderful," he says, and then he waits. I think he's expecting me to turn toward Danny. Maybe he thinks the two of us should greet each other, like long-lost buddies or something, but it doesn't happen. Danny doesn't even so much as acknowledge my existence. Instead, he asks from behind me, "May I go?"

"Certainly," Mr. Murphy replies, without batting an eyelash. And this is where I start to get suspicious. I start to wonder how coincidental this coincidental meeting can be, because Mr. Murphy never lets anyone get away with this level of rudeness. "But first—" He grabs me by the shoulders and spins me around so that I am facing Danny (who is staring at the floor). "Why don't you two go back inside my classroom and catch up, for old times' sake? This will give me time to grade your essay, Danny. I'll only be a few minutes."

Then he confirms my suspicions by shoving the both of us back into the classroom with his massive man-hands (which until this very minute, I never knew he had) and shutting the door quickly behind us.

It's so obvious to me what Mr. Murphy's up to, and I'm pretty sure it's obvious to Danny, too, because as soon as the door shuts behind us he says, "Ugh!" really, really loudly.

The whole thing is awkward and terrible and so much more. I don't even know what to say or where to begin. I just know that I'm standing in a room with Danny Diaz, and I feel like someone keeps spinning me round and round and round.

And the spinning doesn't stop until something happens that makes it all not seem SO awful. I realize that for the first time in a long time, I'm completely stressed out BUT I don't feel a twitch or a panic attack coming on. I just have a really big headache.

"Danny—" I know it's totally silly for me to think that I'll say his name, and he'll look up at me, but I do. Instead, he moves farther away from me, so that he's leaning against Mr. Murphy's desk, staring at his fingernails.

I decide to try again.

"Danny?"

But it's worse this time, because this time he says, "I don't want to talk to you." And he still doesn't look up. He doesn't move.

"Danny?" I say again, because how much worse can it get? But it does get worse. It gets a lot worse, because this time, he practically shouts, "God, Susie, can't you just leave it alone? I can't—" And then he looks up at me, and I see all the hurt I've caused him, every last bit of it, right there in his penny-colored eyes.

He holds my stare until I look away. I don't know what to do, so I move back in the room, until I'm practically in the back row. I brace myself with the help of a desk, and I try not to cry (which I really, really want to do). And all I can think about is how it all got started right here in this room. I think about the day that I met Danny, first in the yearbook line and then here, in Mr. Murphy's classroom. Then I think about everything that's happened to me since— standing up to girls like Tamara and Jessica; making friends with Marc again; growing closer to Leslie and Marisol; and, most important, getting my dad back—and I realize that if it weren't for Danny coming into my life and making me feel something when I had gotten so used to feeling nothing, none of that good stuff would have happened.

"Danny?" I say, and this time I know it can get worse. I'm expecting him to yell and scream. I'm expecting him to stomp right out of Mr. Murphy's room. I'm expecting something big, but I don't care because I have something important to say, something that he has to hear.

It's hard, but I force myself to move closer to him. When we're only a few feet away from each other, I start talking fast. I'm afraid he's going to stop me. I want to get it all out before Mr. Murphy gets back. "Danny, I'm—" I try to will my voice from shaking, but it won't stop. I start again, "Danny, I'm, I'm, I'm so . . . so . . . sorry. I'm so sorry—" And it's here that I start crying. I start crying hard, only I don't care because the tears are honest, the tears are me not hiding, and I think it's time that Danny finally got a chance to see all of me, the real me.

The words are coming out, but they're jumbled and barely coherent. Still I keep pushing forward. "I—the thing is—I haven't been able to feel anything for a really, really long time. And then you came along, and you made me open up, and feel so much more than I ever thought I could. And I wanted to be the way that you thought I could be, but I just wasn't ready yet. I, I didn't know how to let go of all the stuff that had been bothering me for so long, and so I screwed it up. Okay? I screwed it up. And I'm so, so sorry."

It's hard but I force myself to look at him. I force myself to step closer, until we are touching. I say to him, "Danny?" And I reach out to take his hand.

I want him to look at me, but he won't. He's got his chin glued to his chest, but I know that he's heard everything I've said because his hand is shaking just as bad as mine, and he's breathing hard, and I can't tell that it's taking everything he's got not to walk out of this room.

"Danny?" I say again, and I reach out to grab his chin, and tilt his head up so that I can see his eyes. They're sad, but open. It's killing me, but I know I'll regret it for the rest of my life if I don't say it: "Do you think we could . . . ?"

And then I stop because it'll break me if I say it all. It's too much to have everything I want out there, exposed. But I know that he knows what I mean. How could he not, with me standing here, me holding his hand, cupping his chin, and crying so hard that my tears are falling onto his arm? How could he not know what I mean?

He knows. I know he knows because slowly he tucks his chin back into his chest, and he slides to the left so that the only parts of us that are still touching are our hands. Slowly he looks up at me, and his penny-colored eyes appear empty. He says, "I can't—"

"But—" I'm fighting, can't he see how hard I'm fighting for us?

"No, don't. I can't. You don't get it. I don't trust you anymore, Susie. I wish I did. You don't know how bad I wish—" He stops. He tucks his chin back into his chest, and his shoulders cave in. I think maybe it's a sign that he might cave in to me, but he doesn't. A second later, his shoulders are squared and he's looking me dead in the eye. His eyes are hard. And then he's gone, leaving me alone and broken in the vacant room.

# junior year: a new beginning

• • •

"do you have that thing that does that thing?" marisol gestures to me frantically. She's blow-drying her hair with one hand and scrunching it with the other.

"This?" I toss her my eyelash curler. After ten years of being someone's best friend, you understand what she means when she refers to "that thing that does that thing."

"Thanks," she mutters and abandons her blow drying for a temporary bout of eyelash curling.

Over the course of the summer, Leslie took us aside and said that she had been neglecting us—thus began our weekends of makeover madness. The first thing she did was sign us up for a joint subscription to *CosmoGIRL!*, *Teen Vogue*, and *Seventeen*.

"Not for the articles," she said, "but because you girls have to learn how to put makeup on." Then she lectured us on the origins of beauty—how it comes from within; how you should never conform; but, in the overall scheme of things, nothing beats having a great hair/makeup/clothing day.

Then, she took us on a grand shopping spree. And I swear, she was trying to conform us, even if she didn't know that she was.

And maybe we were conformed. And maybe we weren't. Even with all the right clothes in my closet, even with the right makeup on my face and my hair freshly straightened—I don't feel any better about taking another yearbook picture. I still feel raw. Maybe I'll always feel that way.

"How do I look?" Marisol turns around and gives me her mother's smile. It's crazy, but sometime over the last year, Marisol morphed into one hot butterfly.

Unfortunately, my appearance hasn't changed that much. Even with my utterly straight hair, I'm still a funny-looking girl with a hawk nose, fleshy lips, and long limbs. But for some reason, none of that really bothers me anymore. Well, not that much anyway. It's like instead of growing into the butterfly, I grew into my own skin.

"Girls?" My father peeks into the room and smiles. "Wow." His eyes shift from Marisol to me, and his smile grows wider. "You two look really beautiful."

"You think?" Marisol sneaks a look in my full-length mirror and grins. She looks . . . happy. I guess that's what love and a pair of two-hundred-dollar Lucky jeans do to a girl. For the last eleven months she's been a walking glow stick. I have to say that her relationship with Ryan is pretty wonderful. He's kind, considerate, blah, blah, blah—basically, all the things that I wish I had found in a boyfriend. I'm not jealous, though. Well, not that much.

"Are you two ready?" my dad asks.

"Yeah, Dad, I think so. Is Marc here yet?"

Marisol gives me a look. She's not too happy that I'm celebrating the privileges of having my new/old car (Dad finally retired the old Dodge to me) by offering to give Marc a ride to school. But you know what? I don't care. Sometimes you have to go with your gut. My gut tells me that my friendship with Marc is a good thing.

Once Marc and I got our true feelings for each other sorted out, I knew that I wanted him to be my friend, and that he needed my friendship. BADLY.

Besides, after my father told Marc's mother about Marc's extra-curricular marijuana usage, Marc has become a lot more fun to hang out with. He still smokes pot—don't get me wrong—but not as much, not nearly as much.

"Yep, he's been waiting for the last ten minutes." My father consults his watch. "You do know, you're going to be late."

"Really?" This year I have music first period, and I hate to be late. I grab my book bag off my bed, toss my guitar in its case, and pull Marisol from the mirror. "Let's go, golden girl."

as it turns out, we are exactly ten minutes late, but my music teacher lets me slide on account of the fact that he likes me so much. He says, and I quote, that my songs "have real potential."

Real potential. Hearing things like that makes me want to explode with pride. I think he knows that because ever since our conversation, he's been extra-nice to me and I've worked extra-hard to make him proud.

School this year isn't so crappy. My schedule's pretty cool:

1st period—Music, followed by homeroom.

2nd period—Creative writing with Mr. Murphy (still love him).

3rd period—English.

4th period—Lunch. Thank God, Marisol and I still share that time slot.

5th period—Anatomy.

6th period—Calculus, which isn't so bad, but it could be better.

I guess the worst part of my schedule is that I have thousand-watt Tamara in my anatomy class, and every day I have to sit and stare at her notebook that says *I LOVE DANNY* in like a dozen places. They've been a couple since February, and I have to say that just the thought of it makes me nauseated, but I'm trying to be okay with it, really I am. I mean, I lost Danny fair and square, right? It's not really Tamara's fault. She's an opportunist for sure, but our breaking up wasn't really her doing. I did that all by myself.

Still, I wonder. Sometimes late at night, I think, maybe just maybe? I guess a girl can dream. A girl can always dream.

during homeroom we file down to the library to have our yearbook picture taken. I escape my line and wait for Marisol next to the bathroom.

"What took you so long?" I ask when she arrives ten minutes later. "My class is probably done with their pictures by now."

"Sorry, but Mandy decided to hyperventilate right before Mr. Jason dismissed us. So of course, everyone was all concerned, and I couldn't be the only person running out of the classroom."

"Okay. So are you ready?" I take a deep breath and try not to think about last year.

"Yeah, you?" Even Marisol seems a little nervous.

"Yep."

"Okay, let's do it."

We walk toward the library, heads held up high. We are determined to have a decent set of pictures in this year's yearbook. It seems like that's what we've worked toward the entire summer—my being able to smile confidently into the camera. And I think I have a good shot at it, until I walk into the library and see HIM.

"Oh my God. I don't think I can do this." I want to run out of the library and hide.

"What? Who is it?" Marisol surveys the library. "Oh my God." She's as stunned as I am. "I don't think this has ever happened before."

But it is happening, I think. As surely as I am standing here, it is. There he is looking at me with his mouth crumpling into a grimace, Fred, the I'll-take-it-until-you-smile-happily photographer.

"You know what?" Marisol grabs me by the shoulders and gives me a shake. "It's going to be okay. You're going to get into that line and you are going to get in front of that ugly green screen that God knows why they have picked as a background, and you are going to smile. You're going to smile just like we practiced all summer. That's what I think."

Marisol smiles at me encouragingly, and I can't help but feel like I felt the first day of kindergarten when my mom had to promise me that she'd come visit me during lunch, just so I'd have the courage not to cry when she left me.

"You think?" I whisper.

"Yes, I do." Marisol nods at me and exhales deeply. "I do."

I step into the line. I try to tune out Fred and the poor protesting freshman whom he's badgering into giving a glowing smile. I think of Molly Ringwald in *Sixteen Candles*. I tell myself that this experience is not going to be worse than being at a dance where no one decent asks you to dance. I'm just getting my picture taken, that's all. No big deal. And then before I know it, I'm there.

I'm at the precipice of the line. Fred is anxiously staring at me, and I remember how last year he made me twitch, and how Billy Wilson made fun of me for not being able to smile, and how Danny stood there and watched the whole thing and said when no one was looking, "Just smile, Susie." And suddenly I feel calm. I feel extremely calm.

"Okay, mean photographer guy." I take a step forward and center myself in front of the ugly green screen. "I'm ready."

"Excuse me?" The photographer stares at me like I'm crazy.

"I'm ready. We're doing it my way this year. We shoot it once; we shoot it quick. We shoot it now." I smile very widely and count to ten. As if on cue, the camera clicks and flashes. And then I'm shuffled along in the line. I look back to Fred. He's staring after me in utter amazement.

Back in the line, Marisol is suppressing a giggle, but when our eyes meet, she winks at me and mouths, "That was amazing."

"I know," I mouth back. "Can you believe—"

"Excuse me, young lady," a voice snaps from behind me, "but either sign up for a photo package or return to your class." I turn around to find Mrs. Fingle, the assistant principal, glaring at me.

"Oh, sorry," I mumble. Contradicting Fred is one thing, but taking on Mrs. Fingle is another.

I grab my backpack and search around for my order sheet. My father wrote me a check this morning. I wave at Marisol before turning back to the ordering table, and then I see HIM. The other HIM.

Sitting right in front of me is Danny Diaz.

"Hi," he says.

"Hi." Somehow, on some level, I knew that it was inevitable that we would run into each other. I actually fantasized about it numerous times, but there is nothing absolutely nothing to prepare me for the way I feel right now.

My palms are suddenly sweaty. My face is flushed, and my heart feels like I've digested ten Red Bulls in a row.

"Your form," he says, extending his hand out to me.

"Oh, yeah." I limply hand him the form. Our hands touch briefly. We both pull away so quickly that the form falls onto the table.

"Danny?"

It takes a few seconds, but then he says, "Yeah?"

He picks the form up and pretends to look it over. "I have to look busy or Ms. Fingle will have a cow."

"Okay." I take a deep breath and try to think of what I want to say when I realize that the only thing left to say is the one other thing that I've been practicing all summer, which is this: "Thank you. Thank you . . . for everything."

"Oh." Danny stops fiddling with the form and looks at me.

It seems as if we're standing there for minutes when Mrs. Fingle's voice booms behind me.

"Is there a problem in this line?"

I look over my shoulder. Ten students are shifting anxiously, waiting for their turn.

"No, there's not a problem," Danny says. He hands me the receipt. "There are no problems at all. Here's your receipt." He smiles at me, and I remember how I loved his smile.

"Thanks." I smile back.

"Oh, and Susie," he says, as I turn to walk away, "save me a picture, okay?"

# Berkley Jam
# delivers the drama

### Rich Girl: A BFF Novel
by Carol Culver

A new semester is beginning at Manderley Prep,
where being wealthy doesn't make you popular—
but it certainly opens doors...

### Violet by Design (Available March 2008)
by Melissa Walker

The lure of international travel draws Violet back into
the glamorous world of modeling, and all the drama it
brings with it.

### Twisted Sisters (Available April 2008)
by Stephanie Hale

Aspen Brooks thought that college would be a
dream—but between investigating a student's disap-
pearance and fending off her boyfriend's roommate,
who insists he's in love with her, it's turning out to
be one big nightmare.

Go to penguin.com to order!

Turn the page for a special preview of
Carmen Rodrigues's next young adult title . . .

# a little something

*Coming July 2008 from Berkley JAM!*

# Danny and
# the Homecoming Dance

· · ·

thirty minutes later, marisol sends the boys off to get us some cokes from the "bar." When they're gone, she turns to me and gives me a devilish smile.

"What?" I know that smile and it means trouble. "What, Marisol?"

"Nothing." Her voice is clipped, and I can tell that she's trying to suppress her laughter.

Now I'm paranoid. I start to rub at my nose. It's a good possibility that I've got a booger and all Marisol intends to do about it is stand there laughing at me.

"Your nose is fine," Marisol says smiling. "It's not that."

"Then what?" I hate when people tease me. I'd rather they just tell me what it is and get it over with.

"I've got something for you." She reaches into her purse and takes several minutes to produce whatever it is that she is planning on torturing me with. "Here," she says and she hands me a blank three-by-five square that has a glossy surface.

"What is it?" I'm hesitant to grab it from her hand. After so many years of being taunted by other students, I've learned better than to trust anyone with a smirk on their face, even if that anyone is my best friend.

"Flip it over." Marisol thrusts the ominous square into my hand and then waits patiently for me to grip onto it. "Go on," she says.

I look at her eyes, like they might give me a clue as to what might be on the other side of this tiny little square. But she's got her poker face on and I know the only way to solve this mystery is to flip the square, so that's exactly what I do. I flip the square.

And there on the other side, is the glossy version of me. "My school picture?" I look up at her like she's crazy, which I think she just might very well be. "Why are you giving me my school picture? I already have like a hundred of these." Ever since we got back our school pictures several weeks ago, I had been racking my brain for people that I should hand them out to, but the list never grew greater than seven, and I had like forty pics to give out, including several eight-by-tens. I couldn't think of anyone besides my dad and my half-blind grandparents that might want an eight-by-ten of me.

"Well, you promised Danny that you'd save him a picture, and I knew he'd be here tonight, so . . . you know, I thought I'd speed up the process." Again, she gives me that devilish smile of hers, only this time I want to claw it right off her face.

"You're kidding, right?" I thrust the picture back at her like it's setting my hand on fire. "You're kidding, Marisol. Tell me, you're kidding."

"No," Marisol says, rather firmly, "I'm not. Now you can go over there"—she juts her chin in some general direction beyond my shoulder—"and give it to him, or I can. But if I go over there, there's going to be no one to keep Tamara occupied while she's in the bathroom, which"—Marisol stands—"is where I believe she is going right now. So . . ." Marisol looks down at me and places the picture on the table in front of me. "Go." Then she stalks off toward the bathroom.

The picture.

From the top of the table the picture stares up at me accusingly, and I swear it's like a smaller version of me chastising me. I can almost her my mini-me saying, "Well, you did promise Danny a copy of your picture. And he did say, Susie, save me a picture. So what are you so afraid of? Wasn't one of your new school year resolutions to be less afraid? So go be less afraid."

"Shut up," I hiss at my one-dimensional self before I realize that I have, once again, actually spoken out loud.

Great. Now, I'm talking to myself at the homecoming dance. That's attractive, especially because even if I weren't talking to myself out loud, I'm sure my eyebrows were fluttering up and down and my shoulders rolling left to right as the thoughts passed through my head.

Cautiously, I turn around in my seat and scout the room, looking for Danny. It's not like I'm going to give the picture to him or anything, but I at least want to know where he is, in case he's watching me have an argument with myself.

After a few seconds, I spot him leaning against the walk talking to his twin sister, Dalia. I'm just about to swivel back around in my seat when Dalia and I make eye contact. She smiles and waves at me— God only knows why she is waving at the likes of me, because she is the most popular senior at the school—and I have no other choice but to smile and wave back.

I'm frozen in that position—of smile/wave—when Danny turns to look over his shoulder directly at me. Maybe it's the way he smiles at me that causes me to stand. It's like even though there's a good distance between us, his penny-colored eyes can always draw me in. Danny Diaz could be in Africa, and if he smiled in the general direction of America, I might swim the Atlantic Ocean just to be near him. So what was a couple hundred feet in a ballroom packed with kids?

Not much, especially when Danny decides to meet me halfway.

"Hey," he says, when our smiles finally collide.

"Hey." The DJ suddenly stops spinning, and in the sudden silence that precedes the next slow dance, my voice sounds unnaturally loud. I say, "Hey," again, rather awkwardly, and then look down at Danny's feet. He's wearing gray-and-white Converses, and this catches me so off guard that I laugh out loud.

"What's so funny, Susie?"

I don't know what it is, but whenever Danny says my name, I want to melt. I could melt into the carpet or the table or maybe into the fibers of his two-hundred-dollar suit, but melting is most definitely required when I hear Danny say my name.

"It's you—your shoes," I stutter, looking up slowly to meet his eyes. "I think they're great."

Danny smiles at me. It's this slow, gradual smile that he's given me a dozen or more times, but this time, it's like it's the first time I'm seeing it, and I feel a gradual blush crawling up my cheeks. "Me and Tam had a twenty-minute fight over my shoes. I still think she's pissed."

He and Tamara had a fight? OH MY GOD! YES!

"Is that your yearbook picture?" Danny looks down at my hand, which I had half extended to him as we came together.

"Oh," I look down at the object in my hand like it's a complete surprise to me, too, and then I mumble, "Yeah, remember you asked for one? Um, in the picture line."

"Yeah," Danny says, taking it out of my hand and holding it up to the light. He stares at it for a couple of seconds, then flips it over and stares at the blank back. "You didn't write anything on it."

"Oh." I look down at the empty white space, and I don't really know what to say, so I don't say anything.

"That's kinda the best part," he says, handing it back to me.

"Oh, you don't want it, then?" I take it back from him, and when our fingers touch, my stomach (like always) does a flip. Would this guy ever stop having such a strong effect on me?

"No . . . I didn't say that." He shakes his head and cocks an eyebrow at me, and I remember the first time we met in Mr. Murphy's classroom more than a year ago. He was so cocky that I couldn't stand him. I didn't know then how much I would grow to love him. "I just want you to write something on the back and then give it to me later."

"Later?" I swallow hard. Did he mean, like, later tonight? Later at his house? Later when? *When was later?* "Um, like tonight?" I nervously bite my lip.

"No . . ." he says, really slowly, and I start to wonder if he's enjoying my discomfort because he's dragging his words out at a painful pace. "Um, I don't know." He stops to think. "Maybe . . ."

Behind him, a big, blurry object is waving something, and so while he's still thinking (and believe me, he's really thinking), I stare at the object until it comes into focus, and I see that it's Marisol, standing with Ryan and Marc. She's holding a drink in her hand and waving frantically toward the left side of the ballroom. My eyes follow the direction of her hand, but not quickly enough because by the time I realize she's pointing toward Tamara, Tamara is busy tapping Danny on the shoulder and giving me a wicked look.

"How about—" Danny starts a second before impact, but stops abruptly the second he turns around to see Tamara, smiling sweetly beside him.

"Hey, baby," she says, and then she leans forward and tries to give him a kiss on the lips, but Danny turns his head, just slightly, and the kiss lands on his cheek.

"Hey." Danny shuffles on his feet, and then looks to me and smiles apologetically.

"Hi, Tamara." I'm not about to be rude and not acknowledge her. We've known each other since elementary school (her dad works with my dad at the University of Miami) and (because the gods clearly hate me) we also sit across from each other in anatomy. So even though she was the snitch who told Danny about my unplanned/drunken hookup with Marc last year (which is my biggest regret ever), and even though she pounced on him the minute we broke up (if you could even call it a breakup, 'cause it wasn't like we were really going out), we were still officially pretending to be friendly. Because if high school taught you anything, it taught you how to be 100 percent fake.

"Hey, Susie." Tamara turns on the wattage, practically blinding me with her brilliant smile. It's one of the things I hate about her—her brilliant smile. I also hate the fact that her hair is as beautiful as Jennifer Aniston's (nobody in high school should have hair like J.A.'s—that's just unfair), and that she's a homecoming princess, and that she's junior class president. But the thing that I hate the most about Tamara is the fact that she has Danny. I don't know what he sees in her, other than the fact that she's pretty, popular, and smart. I guess that's important to some guys. I just hoped stuff like that wouldn't be so important to Danny. But apparently it is, because if it weren't important to Danny, he wouldn't be here with Tamara. Right?

"So—" Tamara's voice is saccharine. "You're here with Marc? Marc Sanchez? *Right?*" Tamara gives me a pointed look, and I know what she's trying to do. She's trying to sabotage my first decent conversation with Danny in nine months. She's saying, *Remember, Danny? Marc is the guy that Susie cheated on you with. Remember?* And he does remember because the minute he hears Marc's name, a look comes across his face. The look is fleeting, but I see it, and Tamara must have seen it, too, because she smiles victoriously at me. Then she places her hand underneath the crook of his elbow and leans forward to whisper something softly in his ear. He nods, and then she turns to me and says in that oh-so-annoying, particularly condescending voice of hers, "We've got to get back to our table now. They'll be introducing the homecoming court soon. You know how it is."

"Yeah," I say, looking at Danny, who is staring everywhere but at me. "I guess I should get back to my table, too."

"Well . . ." Tamara tucks her hand into Danny's. "Bye." She gives me a wave of dismissal, but I don't move. I'm stuck, watching her holding on to him. My him. And I'm waiting. I'm waiting for Danny to say good-bye to me.

Only when he does finally say good-bye, I wish I had left because his voice is listless and his face lacks any expression. And this time, hearing him say my name is more heartbreaking than anything else.